MW01007421

Field Guide to Outdoor Erotica

Solstice Press

"Field" by Olga Broumas was orginally published as "Field Poetry" in *Calyx*. "Fish" by Charlotte Mendez was originally included in a chapbook published by Serpent and Eagle Press in 1984. "Golden Trout" by Pierre Dellatre was orginally published in *Pendragon*.

A Solstice Press book produced at North Country Book Express, Inc., by Melissa Rockwood, Karla Fromm, Patty McCauley, Carol Loranger, and Jennifer Brathovde under the direction of Patricia Hart and Ivar Nelson.

Edited by Rob Moore
Cover photograph by David Stoecklein
Back cover photograph by Marion Roth
Designed by Melissa Rockwood

ISBN: 0-932722-11-3
10 9 8 7 6 5 4 3 2 1

Table of Contents

Foreword

When we first conceived of this collection, we were unsure what kind of stories (or how many of them) we were likely to get. Would writers respond to our solicitations? Was this idea interesting to anybody outside our office? Would we get stories which were well written, non-sexist, sensual, and erotic?

Overriding these concerns, though, was another question: what *is* erotica?

We knew what it was not: for our tastes, anything involving children, violence, or oppression was emphatically beyond the boundaries. Also, given the outdoor nature of the collection, we thought it wise to specifically rule out bestiality. Whatever we were looking for, we knew it didn't lie in the realm of interspecies hanky-panky.

With these guidelines established, we sent a solicitation letter to dozens of writers, mostly resident in the West but (as is often the case with writers) many of them peripatetic throughout the country. At first only a few stories trickled in, then the trickle became a torrent. Some of the stories were excellent, some were workable, and some were downright strange.

Good writing didn't necessarily guarantee acceptance: some fine stories were just not erotic, and some excellent erotic stories never ventured outside four walls and a ceiling. One story we particularly liked, which with humor and imagination explored the complexity of a peculiar relationship, only stepped into the out-of-doors for a moment: the opening scene featured the protagonist, nude with a chaise lounge strapped to his back, wandering around at dawn on the lawn of a suburban apartment. After that great intro, the action reverted to the confines of the apartment for the duration of the story. Regretfully, we decided that we just couldn't reconcile it to our format, so sent it back.

But some of the stories, perhaps one out of three or one out of four, fit all our criteria. They had character, voice, intriguing situation, an outdoor setting, and, most importantly, they were sensually awake.

These stories began to establish the range of the collection, and in doing that began to define our sense of what constitutes erotica. Some stories moved open-eyed through a world of wonder, of curiosity, a world in which pleasure is cautious, climax discreet. These stories were mostly about the kaleidoscope of feeling that leads to sexual awakening and acceptance, more involved in the heat lightning on the horizon than in the exhilaration of the storm itself. With other stories you were drenched immediately, soaked to the skin, lightning striking everywhere around you. A few were more concerned with the ways that people deal with each other after the storm has passed and the ground is damp, replenished, while others showed more interest in the environment than they did in the characters that moved through it. Some stories worked at a slow boil, others blew the lid off the kettle. Some stories had a very natural premise, worked in a world which we'd recognize, and some happened in wild mystic reaches of the writer's imagination, a place we might not inhabit, but would be glad to visit.

Poems and shorter selections began to take an important place. After twenty pages of lust on the rocks, a poem or a quick humorous scene comes as a welcome relief.

And so the book took shape, selecting itself, in a way, as certain stories fell naturally by the wayside and others fell as naturally into place. We tried not to duplicate themes; when stories seemed too closely related, we'd cull to let the stronger one have room. Even at the end, as the book was being designed and set, as the proofreading and pasteup commenced, all the laborious processes of making a book ready to go to press, we kept our eyes open for the story that still approached the subject from a new direction, that offered another interesting, compelling, and entirely human insight into what individual women and men find erotic. As a few final stories rounded out the collection, we realized how rich the materials really were, how fascinating the variety.

As the saying goes, we got lucky.

We hope you're as pleased as we are by the results.

Rob Moore
Editor

Green Flash

Terry Lawhead

I had her naked and laughing on a bed of ferns when she rolled away and crouched on her knees, saying she knew where an abundant growth of orchids hung down not far from us. Her eyes were shining when she said she wanted to put orchids on my body, and she reached out and lightly touched me again, turning her fingers gently, squeezing. She stood and backed up into the dense foliage behind her, with a provocative, teasing smile I couldn't read, her breasts swaying, and was gone. I lay my head back down and looked up into the lights fusing with delicate palm trees. The sun was low over the sea somewhere behind me and the light here was touched with pinks and reds. As always, it seemed unreal to lie naked and comfortable on the ground in the warm twilight. I recalled her straddling me moments before, smiling to herself, finding little areas within herself to thrust against, searching her own body with my body, aiming me, nodding her head rhythmically as if listening to music....

I sat up. Then stood up. Then ran. She was not coming back. I had been fooled again, she was heading for the beach. I tore wildly through the undergrowth, running full speed on the flat ground toward a jewel of a sun piercing the lush jungle. She would not miss a chance to see the rare green of the sun when it sets on the horizon of the sea. I should have remembered that about her, I should not have let her roll away....But I grinned as I ran, finally laughed loudly, thinking of her passions, how lucky I am when she turns to me.

I pounded across sand that was as soft and warm as an unmade bed after lovemaking, and saw that she was in the surf, sleek arms poised to dive. She disappeared under the breaking wave as I crashed into the water and ran, then dove, too. The water was the temperature of my body and transparent as silk. I knew where she was and swam deeply beneath the breakers. My own desire was the magnet; I pulled strong, grateful for my powerful shoulders and arms, and saw the silhouette of her swimming body. I overtook her, grabbed an ankle, then a leg, and embraced her from behind. She didn't resist, in fact clutched my arms and locked her legs in mine, and we floated for a moment peacefully, my hardening penis snug in the crack of her rump, my lungs full of air. Her long hair floated lightly, like blond pennants at the festival. Small fish flickered at the edge of sight, almost invisible flashes of color. I could hear the whales singing off in the deeper water, could feel their calls shuddering in my body.

We came to the surface and found we could stand, the water was to my chest. She slid her legs around my waist and put her chin on my shoulder. I almost fell when she pushed, her pelvic bones embraced my genitals like the jaws of an immense snake. She slipped one hand down my back to my rump and held me hard, pushing and lifting, probing again for a secret only she knew.

I backed into shallower water where I could stand more easily. A breaker cascaded around us, soft, white and foaming, and we kept our feet. She slipped her free hand beneath her and held me, riding my body like a saddle, and I suddenly knew, with a magical conviction, that as long as I didn't let her touch the ground the sun would not set, that I could keep the sun on the horizon blazing bright green and red for days if I did not let her down.

She understood, and was able to turn me so she could face the horizon. I backed into deeper water again, and she slipped away from me but hung onto my shoulders from behind, turning me to face the sun now just touching the sea and flattening slightly. She put her tongue into my ear, a hand between by thighs and a hand on the nipple over my heart, perching like a monkey, legs wrapped on my hips. The air and sea were one and the sun was hypnotized by our pleasure. One brilliant white sail showed far out at sea. The jungle was empty except for the tranquil birdsong of dusk high in the trees.

She pushed away and began running through the water! I lunged but missed, my hands running down a long slick thigh. Holding my swollen, aching penis in one hand like a lance I splashed after her. She kept her eager face, lit in beauty and tenderness, toward the sun. She wasn't running to escape but just to feel her body pound on the sand once again, to tease the sun. To tease me. I was on her again, now, too hungry this time, bumping her to her knees, my body wanted her warm refuge surrounding me, her hard embrace. I raised her out of the water, holding her rump as if it were a melon and rammed her onto me. She cried out but fell forward in an embrace, beginning to move slowly on me. I felt home again, in the frame of her body.

Then faster. The sun had descended quickly, only the last glowing edge remained, but it was there that the green light would emanate, it was that moment I could sustain. Faster. She rotated on me, rising and falling like the sea itself, not pausing, clinging to my sides as if we could both fall apart, as if this were an earthquake moving our bodies toward each other which could topple us over. She threw her hair back, glistening and smooth, and twisted side to side to see the sun.

One second there was nothing and then there was the flash of green. We felt it inside and involuntarily thrusted, penetrating deeper than ever before, bathed in an unearthly light. She was completely open to me, an orchid peeled back revealing colors never seen, the last moment of the last wild bird on the planet, and I was lost inside of her, with an unlimited vista and endless country to trek. Helpless. Crying for her to not stop. The green lingered, we were keeping the sun up in space over the sea, the white surf was backlit and the distant sail blazed in space. If she had let go of me she would have flown a thousand yards on her back, we were coiled like massive springs, but she held on, pounding, keeping the sun in the sky, the key secure in the wet lock of the world, palm trees glowing in the light on the shore as the green light passed through them like fireworks. I was the prow of a ship at the edge of known things, rocking.

But the sun was placing a heavy weight upon me, the galaxy was on my shoulders, a tremendous tension grew in the center of my body. It was she, she was growing heavier and sinking into me. I felt the suction of wild seas pouring over the rocks and pulling everything down, cleansing the shoreline and sea bottom, and I was unable to stay on my feet. The green light enveloped the sun completely, a translucent glow of nature. Her hands were hard on my chest, beating me. I could barely breathe, she was moving now at the speed of light and perfectly still, pulling me ever deeper and more firmly, my train was traveling through an endless tunnel at an immense speed, box cars careening off the walls and exploding, there were no turns ahead, only the deeper fall....

When I sailed off the cliff, free and light. There was no collision, no up nor down, the sea was illuminated in the soft light it offered from its depths. A rising column of clouds suddenly were lit pink from beneath as sunlight reflected off of the distant ocean on the rounded planet. White tops, pink belly, billowing. She drove me backward until I fell, the receding water washing over us, cleansing, the sound of waves reminding me of sleeping in our own beds, she dreaming and rolling over onto her back, the sheets lightly slapping against our bare skin, one long warm leg thrown over mine. The murmers of love. She squatted over me, palms in the sand, eyes closed but gazing intently into me through her own body, seeing the light around our captive bodies, pelvic bones crushing me in pleasure again and again, opening and closing and twisting. I felt buried inside of her forever and put my hands lightly on her arms to warn her, to tell her of my incredible love for her. I was sinking away into the warm, wet sand, her body still coming closer, arching over me. And overheard stars came out in the darkening blue sky, one by one.

He Rises to My Name

Loretta Anawalt

He rises to my name, to the sound of me
I to him.
The light of his voice came into my ear.
Like a sharp light
He has spoken.
I will wait for him
In the river of my being where there is no darkness
Light touches everywhere the leaves,
the wings of brown birds
In the land, the crabs that feather the rocks.
I will wait for him, my naked body
Joined with the sweet breeze
    that blows from the god's lips.
My hair will flow like honey in the whole light.
I will lie down and I will lie down for him.
My thighs will be as the twin log
    that parts in the forest glen.
He will go in.

My thighs will be the secret joint he enters.
He will open them.
My mouth will be as the opening from which the
    sweet waters stream down the mountain side.
My mouth shall be as the opening of the great river
    that flows.
My fingers shall be to him as the rivulets that caress
    the rocks, the shores, tender sticks
    caught in the eddies.
Yes, my fingers shall come down on him.
I will make myself a river for him where life begins.
I will be long for him and I will be wide
As wide as the mountain where he comes
Searching to find me in the thicket.
I will go down with him
A river I will carry him to the sea to the secret places
Where the gods live,
    to the place beneath the deepest waters.

Rhyme

Julia Bowen

Overhead, a hawk glided lazily, a silhouette making slow circles in the sky. Diane stretched out on a ledge a few feet from the creek, watching him and feeling her body begin to absorb the heat.

The sun blazed down on her and the rock warmed her back as she lay relaxed, head pillowed on her folded shirt. When she could stand the heat no longer, she rolled over and slid off the rock into the water; the feel of it like silk against her skin. Diane touched bottom, her feet burrowed into sand, and rooted, toes digging deeper. She stood for a moment, long enough to slip out of her bathing suit and fling it toward the rocks, where it caught and fluttered, a red flag. Then she plunged into the current.

From where she entered the creek, the water turned a corner to form a pool in front of three large rocks, then slipped over the rounded tops of these boulders to split into two streams. One of these poured a sheet of heavy water eight feet or more to disappear into a crash of white bubbles and foam, while the other, following a more demure path to the right, slipped in and out of crevices, forming a waterfall higher and wider, yet less powerful than the first. It was this branch of the falls that Diane followed, sliding through the current with the froth, letting the flow of the water take her to the very lip of the falls. She caught hold of the columns of

grey basalt, fitting her hands into the cracks and slipping over the rim until she was going down backwards,
carefully climbing with bare feet and hands, and
tanned, naked body.

As she climbed, she looked around. She had a sense
almost of being stoned; time seemed to slow down, and
the colors around her were intense; the fluorescent green
of the sun through tree leaves, the deeper green of the
pines, a flicker of blue jay in the dense foliage. The air
had that electric light that usually comes before a storm,
but when Diane looked up, the sky blazed back at her a
dense blue.

Thomas watched her for a long time.

It seemed to him that she was familiar with this
place, and with the element of water, much more so
than the other people he'd seen in this time. He looked
again at her, to see if she was that much different from
the ones he'd been watching these last weeks. They were
all in such a hurry and they wore such confining
clothing, like tight, bright skins, oddly decorated
plumage. This one was naked, and seemed intent on
nothing more than climbing down the waterfall.

This 'un, nae, she's no lost her senses like th' others.

Her nakedness disconcerted him. The keyed-up
sense that he'd felt back in the forest, the feeling that
had brought him here, was stronger than ever. Not since
Mab had he felt that odd combination of sexual tension
and heightened perception. Not in this time had he felt
anything even close to that.

For the past weeks he'd been aware only of rush and
hurry, of impatience and a kind of animal hunger. For
what, he didn't know. He didn't know what these people
sought, and he didn't think they did either.

*But this 'un! She knows to look around her, to see
what th' earth has to show, tha's the way to see. Those
gormless idiots boasting about their cities, I dinna see
how they can keep their wits about them wi' a place like*

that to call hame.

This woman's hair and eyes were very dark, almost black, and her hair cut short like a boy's. Not like the women of his time, who wore their hair long.

Tentatively Thomas pulled at his clothing, then on impulse stripped off his clothes and concealed them at the base of a large tree. Approaching her while looking as she did would probably make her more comfortable, he thought. He'd noticed that the people in the crowded cities were made very uncomfortable by his clothes. He thought these people were concerned that no one look out of place. He'd even heard this talked about a great deal. Not looking out of place.

Hell's teeth! He was not only out of place, he was out of time.

He moved through the thicket, and stepped out from behind the aspens that crowded the edge of the lower pool.

Diane reached the base of the falls and let herself slide into the pool, turning out of the current as she followed the curve of the bank.

The hairs on her arms and the back of her neck rose. She turned in a circle, not afraid, but abnormally aware of herself and her surroundings. As she grasped a rock at the pool's edge to pull herself up, a movement caught her eyes. As she looked over, a man came out of the trees. He was smiling, naked, and holding his hand out to her.

Diane let go and slid back into the water, and she rocked gently in the current, watching him.

"I'm called Thomas," he said.

She made no comment, but eyed him, treading water. He was big, perhaps six feet, with a strongly built body. His hair was brown, sun-bleached to lighter streaks, and his eyes were a striking grey-blue.

His voice was low and smooth, his accent strange.

Who in the hell is this nut? "What are you doing

here?" she asked. "Where did you come from?"

He turned, pointing. "Ye see yon grove of white trees. I coom because ye pulled me here. Ye hav' no hurryin' feelin' as the rest of thy kind. Ye hav' the ease of the water an' the trees."

Diane's first reaction was to laugh.

Some line, buddy.

Then she was angry. No one had ever found this place, at least when she'd been here. Might have known there was no place to get away for long.

His face was turned toward hers, his eyes studying her.

"Ye dinna believe me," he said sadly. "Ye think I'm one of your ain folk, or th' devil himself coom to hurt ye." He spread his hands out. "I would'na hurt ye. Look, I'm naked, too!"

Diane still didn't speak, and Thomas held out his hand again.

"At least coom talk to me," he said. "Ye'll be tired swimmin' there. Ye hav' no fins for movin' in the water."

Diane spoke then. "You *are* crazy," she burst out. "And I'd be crazy to get any closer to you! Go away and leave me alone!"

"I'm none crazy," he said. "Then, if I maun show ye who I am, I weel."

Thomas sat on the banks of the creek, silently, his strange eyes intent on her face.

Diane reached for the rocks, after all. She saw Thomas metamorphose into a cougar and a wolf, then a deer, a rabbit, and some kind of otter. She closed her eyes for a moment, but the pictures went on. A raven came down to the water's edge and swooped away with a raucous cry. She saw a beautiful woman and Thomas together, and heard Thomas cry, "Mab, I will na gae!" and the woman's low-voiced answer, "Ye hav' to go, ye canna stay here. Th' devil will choose ye for his seven

year tithin'; he kens it's thee I love th' most." Diane saw
the woman embrace Thomas, and when she pulled
away, she was crying.

"Seven years we've had, an' nae ye maun gae back to
your ain kind. I give ye th' gift of prophecy, a good gift
if ye use it well. Ye canna lie. Take care that people want
th' future e'er ye tell, an' may we meet ag'in, Thomas th'
Rhymer."

Diane felt tears on her face and when she opened her
eyes again, Thomas was very close. His hand came up
and touched her face, touched the tears. Then his mouth
was on hers, light and cool, then again, closer, clinging
and warm, moving down then to the hollow at the base
of her neck. As Diane's thoughts scattered through her
mind into pictures of Thomas making love to her, he
picked her up carefully and carried her away from the
water, into the trees.

This is not me lips on her skin slide silky smooth
down from hollow to hollow *this is impossible who is
this man* hands cup her breasts, a stifled furious
breathing fast and light she recognizes in a daze as her
own Close warm weight *Naked feels good, skin to skin*
sliding *oh yes* his body tense as he enters her *what is this
incredible lassitude* wet my god the wetness threatens to
flood her but he's moving now *yes* the rocking a rhythm
in her matches breathing ragged slick every inch of
her alive to touching his skin smooth his chest a tangle
of fiercely curling hair look *yes* hands fingers into
that tangle down the line to his belly lower circles the
shaft of him where it enters her

oh god yes a moan from him the sensation of being
poised on the edge of waterfall, spray blinds her until
she falls tumbling over and over in the air slides into
the water cool deep and lets go.

Diane opened her eyes to meet Thomas' intent gaze.
"Holy shit," she said. "Who *are* you?"

His eyes never left hers; he smiled.

"I'm called Thomas," he said again. "True Thomas, in my time. An' tho' it sounds like a lie, I'm o'er seven hundred years livin' on this earth. An' tha' is th' truth, lass, I canna lie. I'm a shape-shifter an' I tell what's to coom. An' I tho't I'd never ag'in find a woman such as thee."

Diane pulled away to look at him. "And now what will you do, Thomas the Rhymer?"

His smile grew deeper. "I coom here from ma' oon time, and I could'na gae back, because everywhere I looked, it was dead, th' magic was dead, and th' people did 'na seek it, and I could'na gae back. Now I can. Ye gave me back the road to gae home, an' I do thank thee."

Diane reached for him and he met her halfway with a hug that felt solid and good. He stood, and as he walked into the woods, Diane leaned back on her elbows and watched. At the grove of aspens he turned and she saw him smile, then his human form faded and a buck deer leaped the thicket and was gone.

Sunglasses

Lin Colson

He always wore sunglasses. Lean and about my size in his boots and jeans, he was typical of the men who made up that cattle country. What caught my interest was those sunglasses. Most of the cowboys would squint into the sun their whole lives, letting the white light seep in through narrowed eyelids shaded by cowboy hats. This guy knew the advantages of barriers.

Barriers were a soul theme for me, and what ultimately caused the divorce. After which, I couldn't move. I sat in that city apartment drinking every night and listening to Patsy Cline. It wasn't that I loved him anymore or even cared about that woman he ran off with. It was despair caused by dreams gone bad. Patsy Cline knew about that stuff; Wilma didn't.

"One door closes, another opens," she'd say over the phone.

I knew that, but my heart had an aching hole in it. At first, I'd close my eyes and see the hole. Later, I'd close my eyes and see the hole with the Nebraska sky shining through. When Wilma called to ask me to help out during the hay harvest on the ranch, I went back.

Two years is too long to mourn a marriage. Ten years is too long to be away from land that shaped your spirit. I was happy to be in the sandhills again.

The first time I saw him, I was in the yard hanging out the laundry. He was out of a red pickup and at the gate quickly. When water's the issue, you hurry; but I looked twice before I headed downstairs for the jug. I admit, I like a man who looks like that.

"Thanks. I'm Larry," he said when I returned.

A jolt shot between us.

"I'm Lil."

It'd been years since a man interested me, even my husband. Now a sensuousness struck me whenever I took the meals to the fields. The sandhills will cradle your needs, let you live in the midst of your fantasies. I'd ride the buckskin to the canyon during late afternoons, tying my shirt on the saddle, letting hot winds ride over my breasts and tug at the hole I called heart. On soft grasses next to the spring's pool, I'd watch the sky fill with reds and purples while I tried to understand the moist gurgle. Often I sat in the small pool, sweet water running over my arched body, through my thighs.

We spoke in the easy way of people who are comfortable with conversation. I'd been rooted to the spot, my awareness narrowing to just the two of us. White blond hairs on the sunburned forearms, the full upper lip, aviator sunglasses, a slice of blue harvest dusted sky, my burned cheekbones squinting. I couldn't tell if he noticed the charged air between us. Among other things, age has taught me to appreciate mystery.

We drifted toward each other in that bare, exposed environment. Each of us hidden behind our glasses. We passed information about the world or the harvest as I passed him a sandwich. He began talking about himself, too.

"Went to work in the office of a mining company after college." He was sitting in the shade of the pickup. His glasses reflected my mouth, which looked soft. "Didn't like it. Came back and started following the harvest."

"Lot of time on the road," I said.

"That's what I like," he said. I had to smile.

He brushed a sweat bee off my shoulder. Our glasses reflected the other as we stared into the movement.

I've been around the block, as they say, and try to live an examined life, yet some feelings still confuse me. Sexual intensity is one. It drove me into several beds when I was younger. But the marriage burned something out of me. The intensity was there; but the joy wasn't. No playful surprises where fingers barely touch an exterior. No looking into the other's eyes and letting heart's laughter spill out. The marriage taught me joy is what I need; it was hard to have fun as long as I was considered the source of communion. All my life I've been able to laugh. Now what I want is to laugh deeply and love hard. What I needed was to see this guy's eyes. I needed to see what lived there.

Days passed hot beginning with the meadowlark's calls through my window to where I lay on the sheets in warm disarray, perspiration already skimming my upper lip. Sweat lived on you in the kitchen and in the fields. My clothes clung even as I drove the pickup through heavy harvest air to deliver meals to the field. Harvest was nearly complete. We talked, but rarely touched. In my dreams we touched, skin-on-skin. My lips were moist; my neck exposed.

The rain slashed its way through the final fields. We had to wait for some drying. A red pickup pulled into the yard.

"Lil," he said over the fence. "Let's walk down to the trees and see some birds."

They planted those forty acres of trees to get more free land from the government during homestead days. After a hundred years, most weren't alive and those that lived weren't thirty feet tall. But they hid us from the house and the horizon.

I'm not the kind of woman who can easily approach a man. Call it my Fifties mind-set; call it shyness; call it fear. Once we stepped in, it just seemed like the thing to do. My body was burning and my mind was made up.

Summer heat hung at the edges, but the interior was cool. A meadowlark sang and sang. Sweet grasses bent. The smell of warming pine needles crawled into my mouth. With wind blowing the bugs, I reached out, stopped him, stepped back and stripped off my shirt. Then I unsnapped his shirt, pulling him out of it and so close to me. He stood still for a moment and let me learn my own lessons. Then his arms came around me. And the smell of intensity as strong as pine needles rose out of us.

I told him some things about the marriage and the drinking and the hole in my heart. Other things are best saved for other moments. What we were really doing was trying to get beyond the barriers. Heat wavered the edges.

"Larry," I said. "I need to see your eyes."

He took his glasses off. My heart filled to my ribs. What lived there was as wild and free and fun as Hank Williams in his better days. I put my hand up to his face, to his mouth and he kissed the palm while we looked at each other. What can I say? Desire can sweep over you like a Nebraska wind. We ran and rolled and gurgled. Touched softly. Loved hard. Sweat was a spring all over us. The guy drove me wild. I laughed my ass off.

The Business of the Can Between Us

Diana Armstrong

There were a couple of things I know I did every day. One was to look at the mountains and the other was to look up the river. By those acts I kept time and I kept going. I faced east when I got up—not in a ritual sense, but soon—and when I did I saw the mountains. Then driving east into town to work, when I crossed Corrales bridge I looked upriver.

Always upriver because that was where any changes came from. In the summer the river could be completely dry one day, an inert stretch of sand, then the next roiling bank to bank with muddy water, dotted with thick clods of foam.

In this valley beneath the mountains, the river spreads out. A swath of hopeful trees dogs both sides—the bosque, a tumble of spindly cottonwoods, Russian olives, tamarisks, and willows. It's easy to get to and a lot of people play in it.

Every summer a few boys drown. They walk off into a hole or jump in a place they're sure is deep—it was last time—but it isn't now. No one can see what happens in the umber-colored water.

At the north end of Corrales there is a beach that's popular night and day. The trash of many cervezas litters the sand like peculiar shells of love and boredom.

Wear shoes in the water! mothers tell their children.

We have come to play awhile after work, my girls and I. It's about seven o'clock. They are squealing and splashing and falling down where the water is calm and warm as a puddle. I have walked out into the channel, delighting in the pull of the current on my legs and the wearing away of the sand under my feet. Every once in a while something tiny brushes my leg: it's creepy, not having any idea what it might be. As I walk into deeper water, feeling for big holes that step off into oblivion, the water claims my thighs in a cold advance, like someone making a ring with their creamy hands and sliding them up my legs. When the water surface begins to lap my inner thigh, I face upstream and step wide. I wonder if orgasm would be possible. I concentrate on the licking of the water. But it's too cold. For me, anyway; maybe someone else could do it. I take a step, and the water gains new ground halfway up my butt; lust is numbed. I glance back at the beach. The girls are fine. A man is nearby, looking in my direction. I can't tell without my glasses if he's looking at me, but I think he is because a dog, and it must be his dog since it's leaping toward him through the water with a frisbee in its mouth, is coming from downstream and he's not looking enough downstream to be watching his dog. I've had my foray, I start heading back. My big toe smashes sharply into something. Shit, I should have kept my shoes on. I lean down to give my toes a squeeze and find what it was I ran into that hurts so bad. My fingers catch on a jagged metal edge. Damn people dump their shit into the river. I should move it, a child could really get hurt on it. With my fingers I examine the contours of the object, trying to draw a picture for my useless eyes. I see myself and the river in cross-section; I'm squatting humbly above the fin, perhaps, of a wrecked 1961 Impala. Suddenly it's clear: it's a bulk oil container, one corner sticking out. I find the handle and pull as hard as I can, but it doesn't budge. The current piles the sand back in as fast as I dig it out. What I need is another pair of arms. The man is still on the beach, throwing the frisbee for his dog. I motion for him to come out.

Help me dig something up...it's dangerous! I add the last so he won't expect a treasure.

He high-steps through the river, slim and shirtless, just the same as his dog leaps — easily and with energy. Maybe he thinks I'm in trouble, couldn't hear me say dig something up. It's too late now, here he is in front of me, smiling, and the dog too, his tongue a slash of pink in all the brown of river and tanned skin and dark wet denim of us. He sends the dog back.

I tell him that there's a buried five-gallon can here that's got a very sharp edge and is dangerous for children and should be moved out of the water, but it's too heavy for me, I can't budge it, but between the two of us, I think we can lift it and carry it to shore. I take his hand to lead it down to the can. Suddenly I see things as he must, this woman taking his hand under the water, taking his hand to anyplace. I'm sure that he has already thought of this. He loves this, is happy to go along with this curious seduction. I kneel, he kneels, thank God the can is still there.

If he expected me to place his hand between my legs, he does not show it. There is a cockiness about him, though; he is sure that had I placed his hand between my legs, I would not be disappointed.

The can is between our knees. We are surgeons and it is out patient, we are Cro-Magnon and it is our fire, we are parents and it is our baby.

The river breaks upon his back and wraps around him at solar plexus level. The compromised current then draws a line across the rise of my breasts like an old strapless gown. I reach under the blanket of muddy water and meet his hand that has found the handle.

With his other hand he is trying to scoop the sand away fast enough to get a grip on the other end. I move around beside him to help block the current and sweep away the sand. He pulls on the can, trying to rock it, work it out of the sand. Something—a hand?—travels lightly up my arm and just brushes my nipple. I know it was a hand. I'm truly surprised. But his eyes are down and tell nothing.

We've managed to get a bigger part of the can out of the river bottom and into the river. He sits back on his heels to rest a moment and gives me a warm smile that shoots me in the stomach. My friend Sandy called those thrill shots. Then he lets the smile fade and staring at me, leans over to kiss me. My vulva tingles, the sensation spreads, opening me to him, rising to stop my breath, making me hot and light-headed—and suddenly angry. I turn away and check the shore. I asked him to help me dig out a can. That was what I called him out here for. I don't need this. I give him a hard look meant to pull age on him, meant to remind him that we were moving a can, that I was here with my kids. And it works, below decks the unruliness is subsiding, and he returns his attention to the can.

I move back around in front of him so I can push when he pulls. He is caught up in his contest, concentrating his strength. He has that look of self-absorption, I'd seen on lovers' faces. I feel the can moving, rising, being forced from its river bed, and it seems monstrous. He leans slowly back, then stands, holding across his thigh a blazing, bullet-riddled, bottom-filled, five-gallon can. Water gushes from all the holes. Of course holes, of course bullet-riddled. I run to grab hold of the end without the handle and lock my fingers together under it. The can is hard for me to carry, it bites into my arms, he is much taller, shore seems a long way off.

As the water line goes down, the curtain rises, I feel I am on stage and naked, my body brought to light with the can. My muscle shirt is stuck to me like a second skin, my nipples are hard. My thighs and calves look good from running. I know I look good. His dog bounds out to meet us.

A few feet out of the water and I have to let go of the can. My girls don't tarry long from their games, it's just an old can.

Well, thank you, I say.

We should take it farther back, he says, gesturing with his chin toward the bosque.

My stomach tightens, but he's right, it appears I must carry this thing a while longer. We brush through stick willows and stunted sunflowers and garbage and river grass and enter the belt of weedy cottonwoods, he matching his steps to mine, and finally we heave the ripped silver can, heavy with clay and heavier with civilization, at the base of a tree.

Now the business of the can is finished between us. Now we are out of the water and nothing is hidden. Now we are away from children and dogs. And my nipples are still hard and he is truly half-naked and his levis are slung below his narrow waist. And I begin to talk, talk away the air thick with the smell of evening and willows and the rasp of crickets; talk a hole in the closeness, belittle the carrying together, the current, the island we made in the current, the microcosm of silence and senses we were. I thank and praise him and all this time we have been walking back to the river.

Wait, he says, what is your name?

The sun is perched on the horizon behind us and its last, level rays are split by the thin woods into long fingers of golden light. One of which is pressing against him, covering him, loving him. His voice is nearly a whisper and he places his hand on my arm.

Stella, I say and now I am out of words because of his color, because the late sun has struck him golden, because his chest is scattered with bright water drops and his eyes are the color of bosque, lichen, moss and I can see into them like glass. He holds me with his eyes, tenuous and yearning, and places his hands around my ribs, and with his thumbs, he strokes each nipple. My loins melt, I ache to touch his skin, press against him. I meet his kiss, our parted mouths just grazing, teasing, playing out the breathtaking strangeness of touching each other. He runs his tongue around my lips and kisses my neck, nuzzling and nipping. He turns me around and covers my breasts with his hands and bites the back of my neck. I stretch and arch my back like a cat, wrapping my arms high around his neck. He slips one hand down inside my cutoffs and I step wide, reveling in what he is doing with his fingers. The pleasure is sharp and I pull hard on his neck and arch and press my butt against him. I come so easily, it rolls over me, but what I want is to have him in me, tying us together and filling every space. I swivel out of his embrace and get behind him and draw circles on my open palm with his nipple and slip my hand into his pants. He is hard and hot, I want to get him out of his levis, take him in me, make him come. He groans and takes my hand away. We slip out of our pants and he lays down and I ride him, slow, pulling away to the point of near panic, then taking it back, deeper, more sure. Waves of sensation rolling shore to shore in my body, I feel his orgasm starting, he holds on, locks his arms around me and thrusts hard and I can't tell our feelings apart anymore.

We lay still, our hearts beating close and it returns to me that I have been gone too long, that I must get back, my girls are too young to be left alone, or they may come find us any minute.

I have to go, I say. I hate this part, I hate the separating, I hate breaking the ring we'd made of nerves and limbs and fluid.

A child screams. I recognize my youngest. I step into my shorts and tear back to the beach. The other one yells, Mom!, fear in her voice. They see me running and the little one limps crazily toward me, arms flailing, her face screwed up with hurt.

I'm bleeding, I'm bleeding, I'm bleeding! I kept telling her to stop it, but she kept pushing.

Blood is trickling down her heel. I scoop her up and carry her to the car.

I told you to keep your shoes on!

I set her on the front seat and examine the cut. She's still howling. It's a deep cut, but clean, from glass or a pop top. Butterfly sutures will probably be enough. Except that it's on her heel. Doctors have gone home by this time. I'll ask Connie. I wrap a towel around her legs so she can't see the blood. The oldest hangs back, scared, in trouble again.

Get in!

The little one lays her head on my lap, shaking and moaning. I race up the arroyo road, leaving a tunnel of dust behind me in the glow. In the rearview mirror, I see the man standing by his pickup, his black dog beside him. I watch him watch my car until it bounces over the top of the bluff above the river.

Hot and Stillness
In the Grove

Loretta Anawalt

Hot and stillness in the grove
The men are singing
In the grove below
From the earth below her feet
The men are singing.

The fingers of the sun move in her hair,
    in the tree limbs, in the ground
On the men below.
The men are bronze and gold
They are bronze.

Their song rises like the high fingers of the sun
Shimmering echo, fine as the foil of leaves
It brushes against her arms, her throat,
    ghost of desire it enters her.

She is walking the ground of her spirit.
Her father's song rings
In the tendons of the men
Sings low in the grove
Soil of her nativity
Water song
Stone song
Spirits
They lie hidden from her in the blind grove.

Her feet press the grapes of her father.
The wine is rising, the purple grape
The foam. It flicks her lids
Her tongue
She licks the foam from her lips
    where it rises.

Song of the daughter
She will sing. She will press
    the grapes to her nipples
The wine will flow from her lips
From her nipples, from her red eyes
The sun will heat the wines that flow from her.

She will open the trunks of her hips.
The wine will rush from her,
    from the dark pool where it lies waiting.
It will drown the song of the men that is rising
    with the heat
With the thunder of its coming
It will sweep away the olive and the men.
The grape it will carry with it away
The shimmering leaf. It will displace rock.
The rock it will sunder. It will
Shatter the rock, the shimmering branches,
The men's song. It will wash over them.

Night Eternal

Alice LaBelle

Ann was seeking large spaces, large silences, spaces and silences so big they would reduce her to a speck of dust, a grain of sand, the tiniest of seeds in a vast cosmos. If she could merge with something big enough, important enough, she hoped her passion for Jack would be cut down and made to seem similarly minute.

She arranged to take a few days off from her work as a freelance writer, polished up an article on gardens of the Palouse for *Sunset Magazine* and sent it off. It was full summer, unusually fine weather for June. She headed east into Idaho, the North Fork of the Clearwater, where she and Lou had fished. Familiar territory, wild enough to suit her mood. She drove the dusty ribbon of highway past Jackknife Creek to an old logging bridge. About a mile beyond the bridge she found an isolated sand spit sheltered from the road by tamarack and pine and hulking boulders that looked like giant totems. She could relax and feel free for awhile, shake her demon, she hoped. Strong sensation was the best antidote for demons.

She worked up a sweat setting up her tent, then headed for the water. Stripping naked in the sand, she waded in fast, her tender thighs shrinking from contact with the icy stream. She paused for a minute, crossed her arms over her breasts and shuddered, then she plunged in. "Make myself numb," she thought. When the water hit her full she screamed, breaking instantly into a crawl, heading upstream against the current, then letting the fast water carry her back. She eased herself into an eddy a few feet from shore, flipped on her back and spread her legs wide, kicking. The water swept into her open crotch. The hot sun was full on her face and upraised breasts. It was like being made, so sweetly did the motion of the waves wash up into her.

She peered down into the shadowy waters. His wraithlike figure appeared green and glistening, gazing up at her—so real if wishing could have made it so, he would have risen up from the emerald depths and come into her.

"This is no good," she said, swimming ashore, stumbling out over the rocks. She fell back on her towel, her body and limbs loose. Again she let her legs fall open to the sun. Its heat reached deep into the tender flesh of her inner thighs. She glanced down at her breasts ruefully. Her nipples were upraised and drawn. She stroked them lightly, falling into a reverie. Images of his body flickered through her mind like the swallows darting across the cliff face—his loins, his hips, his lower belly, the honey-colored hair that swarmed over his broad chest, his hands, his fingers, the shape of them, the sweet line of his strong chin. She imagined she was kissing the soft places at the joints of his knees, his instep, his ankle. She sat up suddenly, shaking her head hard. "I'll go mad," she said.

The sun was still high. The air was sweet with pine, mock orange and wild rose fused into a natural aphrodisiac. She plucked a tiny, exquisite birdbill from a cluster growing by her hand. She held it up close, studying its perfection.

"Where is he now?" she mused. Would he come after her? It was the craziest of hopes. She left just enough information on her answering machine for him to figure out where she was heading. She bit her lip and frowned. He was probably still in the Wallowas, at one of those pristine lakes he and Lou loved so much.

She chewed her lip. "I'm a fool," she told herself. She tried to make herself think about Lou, in London. She hoped he was having fun? It eased the guilt. He'd been gone just long enough for her to begin to miss him a little, when she wasn't wanting Jack, forgetting everything but the dream of fucking her husband's best friend.

In the weeks before Lou's departure, she and Jack had kept a careful distance, stepping around each other when he came by. When she couldn't handle being in the same room, she escaped to her studio. Not coming close enough to touch became an almost zen exercise with them. At night, with Lou at work on his text in his study below, in the merciful dark of her bedroom she could surrender to her desire. He glowed before her, stepping naked from the shower, his cock swinging like a sweet rope. Still naked he slipped through the shrouded streets. Magically he climbed the trellis to her window, his legs taut and sinewy, the moon silvering his hips.

They had seen each other naked at a hot springs, when the three of them drove over to Missoula one weekend late in spring for a wilderness conference. Lou was giving a paper. The springs were deep in the Montana woods. They drove over in Jack's pickup, parked by the road and hiked a mile along a deep ravine. At the bottom was a creek they could hear but couldn't see, rushing in a torrent through the blind underbrush. They came to a clearing and climbed the side of the hill to a giant cleft in the rocks where the hot springs flowed. The full moon shot into view, lighting the springs.

When he stripped his clothes away, her heart stopped. He was longer and fuller than any man she'd ever seen, so beautiful she had to lower her eyes for fear Lou would catch her looking.

Afterwards, remembering the way he hung made her half faint. The vision of his naked beauty put her in a trancelike state. It seemed to her almost like a state of grace.

He had watched her, oh how he had watched her, his eyes brushing like gauze over her breasts, the soft lines of her belly, the silky hair of her mound of Venus. She half swooned under the caress of his gaze. She closed her eyes, abandoning herself to it.

Lou was clearing away rocks to make a place for her. She turned her face up to the moon and closed her eyes, reeling with the force of Jack's desire. She opened her eyes. They looked full into each other's face. It was as if they were the first man and woman on this earth, and they had found each other. Her eyes dropped down to his cock. It was rising, straining upward. The curve of it was like a sweet bow in tension. My god, she half whispered, her breath catching in her throat. If Lou had gone away, they would have fucked right there in the spring. They wouldn't have waited to find dry ground.

That night in her memory was a purgatory of unslacked desire. They feasted on each other in the only way they could, with secret, stolen glances. They were in the deepest waters but they couldn't drink.

The ledge basin they shared was too narrow, too confining to allow escape from Lou. Whenever she could, when Lou's attention was elsewhere, she shifted her body ever so slightly to allow Jack full access. She gave herself to him the only way she could. The moonlight touched her breasts with burnished fingers. Her nipples were pierced with sharp pins of sweet sensation. It was as if he were brushing them with his lips, drawing them in, sucking them, biting them.

When they changed places for the men to shift more rock and deepen the basin, his cock brushed against her hip. She was so dizzied she leaned back against the rough cliff. It was the only time their bodies touched. It left a wound in her thigh that burned in the steaming water.

When she could stand it no longer, she got out and walked naked, carrying her clothes down the hill, feeling his eyes on the sloping curve at the small of her back, knowing that he was watching every shift of her hips, every swing of her full breasts. Reluctantly she slipped on the lace undergarments, her skin continuing to burn, drawing her levis on with slow deliberate movements.

On the hike out, it was as if an electric current connected them, binding them in a fine tension. He took the lead, moving ahead of her like a big cat, stealthy and surefooted. He was at home in the woods, at his very best, the finest wildlands management man in the department. There was nothing he didn't know about wilderness. He was a master fisherman, none better with a fly. He didn't talk much. It was hearing Lou go on about him that made her look past his quietness, begin to see into his deep blue eyes that she'd caught watching her.

At the truck, she climbed in between the two men. Lou might as well have been on another planet. All she could see, all she could feel was Jack's presence. His hair was damp and curly from the steam. She longed to reach up and run her fingers through it, to lick his upper lip along the edge of his full moustache, to bury her mouth in his neck. As they sped along the highway to Montana, her hip fused with his and the current shot through them igniting a delicious molten sensation in her vulva that washed up into her belly again and again. He leaned forward and pressed a tape into the deck. She inhaled his scent. The music pounded in her ear, "...and fillin' me up so, that all I need to know, is here you come again, and here I go-oh-oh-oh." Had he chosen Dolly Parton's sweet lament on purpose?

Ann drove back from the North Fork feeling cleansed and refreshed. She'd taken in enough mountain air to clear her head. He hadn't shown, but it didn't matter. He would. Her days on the river gave her the strength to wait.

As she drove the rim of the widening canyon toward

Lewiston, the trees fell away behind her. She entered the knuckled cliffs edging the river like prehistoric beast paws, ageless, colossal, their camel coats shimmering with heat. She populated the bright sky with her love, draped him unclothed over distant cloud banks in full masculine splendor. When the vision began to fade, she replayed his last visit in her mind. It had lost none of its power to shake her.

He'd stayed away, then showed the night before Lou left, striding up the walk, his head lowered, as if he'd made up his mind to something.

Seeing him jarred her. She ran to let him in. Her voice was shaking. "Where have you been?" she asked, as if she didn't know, as if she hadn't struggled against the drumming urge to call him, to drive to his place on any pretext. And then...what? Offer herself to him? Throw herself at his feet?

He looked at her sternly. Her eyes burned hot. She bit her lip and turned, moving ahead of him into the kitchen. Lou was paying bills. They were spread out in confusion on the table. As she passed him, he reached out and circled her hip with his arm, pulling her near. "What a mess," he said, smiling at his friend. He glanced up at her with affection. She bent down and kissed his lips lightly. "Take care of her," he said. "See she doesn't get in too much trouble." He turned back to the bill he was holding. She met Jack's darkened eyes.

The talk centered on London, a welcome distraction. Jack listened intent, curious about the city, how it was laid out, if there were any good trout streams on the island. "Western born, western bred," she thought, deeply pleased.

When Lou left to go upstairs for a few minutes, Ann turned her back to Jack deliberately, moving to the sink to pour herself a glass of wine. She sensed him coming for her like a dark wind. His hands caught her low in the belly, pulling her against him. He moved between her legs, hard and urgent. His mouth was on her neck, her shoulder, biting into the bare flesh. She shuddered. His swift hands slipped up to her breasts, exploring them with open palms, his fingers drawing her nipples to two points and pinching them hard enough to make her wince. He turned her around swiftly, crushing her against his chest, his groin thrusting once, slow and deep. His mouth was full on hers for an instant. She felt her knees dissolving. As swiftly as he had claimed her, he put her away from him, his fingers biting into her shoulders, his eyes angry with desire.

"That's where I've been," he hissed.

She was shaken to her toes. She sighed brokenly, almost a sob. She was afraid to move. If Lou's footsteps hadn't sounded in the hall, she might have dropped to her knees and hung her head before him.

He moved toward the back door. "Send me a postcard," he called.

"Going already?" said Lou, surprised, following him to the door, circling his shoulder in a gesture of farewell. "Leave a few trout for me," he said.

"I'm headed for the Wallowas in the morning," Jack rejoined.

Ann's heart sank. How long would she have to wait?

When she was invited to the department barbeque, she almost didn't go. Enough time had gone by for him to be back. She knew he wouldn't call. One day he'd simply be there, without warning. She lived for that moment.

It was almost dark when she arrived. The house was full of friends and acquaintances, the backyard thronged. The scent of newly mown grass and lingering lilacs sweetened the air. They were roasting a suckling pig to celebrate the first day of summer. When she saw him stride through the gate, her breath stopped in her throat. He'd already spotted her. They circled each other in the crowd, moving like shadows as the moon unfolded from a drifting cloud and the stars opened their white eyes one by one.

The conversation around her was like the droning of bees. His eyes glowed, stroking her face, her eyelids, whispering to her. She moved through a lacework of mock orange toward the gate into the shawl of shadow, her ears keen for the fall of his foot. She felt him almost before she heard him, his arm circling her waist, directing her forcefully, sweeping her toward his truck, their bodies moving in unison. She didn't dare look up, her heart was beating too wildly.

"Dearest," he said, kissing her mouth, her neck, opening the door for her with sure motions. He half lifted her in and closed the door, moving around the truck, swinging with muscular grace into the seat beside her. He took her face in his hands again and turned it to his, kissing her mouth, her eyes. With a stroke he fitted the key in the ignition.

When they turned down into the gulley leading to the old Moscow highway, he reached over and pulled back the thin fabric of her sundress, cupping her crotch and pressing hard. His teeth were clenched. He'd driven the upper road like a man possessed, his neck rigid with purpose. She gripped the seat, beside herself with joy and terror, her mouth half agape.

He pulled in by a clump of tall cottonwoods. They leaped from the truck with the same blind haste that had marked their movements since leaving the party, seeking each other in the sudden dark. Across the field of wheat the lights of a farmhouse blinked. She heard the gurgling of a small creek cloaked by the trees. Drawing her behind him, he made a path through the brush toward a low spot where the moon unmasked a patch of meadow grass. At a barrier of weed and thicket, he swept her in his arms and carried her over, lowering her to the grass. The stream was almost close enough to touch. It rang in her ears.

He was loosening the lace in her bodice, peeling the cloth back, freeing her breasts. He fell to them hungrily, holding each one up like a trophy, kissing them, pausing to look deep into her eyes, then stripping the dress and panties away altogether. On his knees he parted the lips of her cunt, thrusting his tongue in, shuddering.

She was reeling with love. His tongue swept the tip of her clitoris like wildfire. "Stop," she cried, when she could bear it no longer.

She pressed her hands to his ribs. He rose up till they were both on their knees. She was working his belt buckle.

"Let me," he murmured. In an instant his pants and shirt were away, his cock against her cheek, her lips, her mouth opening to receive it full. She tilted her head back for him to see how she loved him. His eyes were on her mouth, the vision burning into his brain. She drew back and sobbed. Her heart was so full. She could scarcely bear the joy of feeling him with her tongue. She wanted to kiss him everywhere, to press her face between his legs, but she needed to look at his cock. They drew back and looked at him together.

He pressed her shoulders down and back, forcing her gently onto the grass, moving down between her legs and thrusting his tongue between her lips, searching for the sweet point. "Oh," she cried, stabbed with sensation. He stopped like an animal who's heard a noise, looked up at her intently. Then his head fell again, his tongue searching, thrusting, caressing. Wave after wave of sharp sensation cut up into her womb. Her legs fell open wide, wider. She couldn't spread them wide enough.

"Turn over," he said, grasping her hips and moving her under him. He was kneeling over her, his cock swinging free and full. She was stunned by the vision, the way she had been the first time she saw him. She felt almost grieved that he wasn't in her mouth again.

She let herself be pulled down. He spread her cheeks and held them apart, looking at her before he began to press the tip of his cock into her. She was so wet he went in full, almost at once. She gasped. He was so big the tip hit hard against the entrance to her womb.

"Did I hurt you?" he asked, pausing.

"No, no," she said. "Don't stop." Rills of sensation were coursing through her. She'd never been so alive to a man's cock. It was as if they were made to be joined. She raised up, arching her lower back, opening her thighs to him.

"Like this," he said, drawing them together, his cock thrusting low and deep. He paused. "I'll come too fast this way," he said, withdrawing, turning her over, kissing her face, pressing his cock against her hip, probing her lower lips with his fingers, stroking her crown till it stood erect and throbbed in response to his touchings.

Slowly he caressed her, moving up till he was centered on the spot and she thought she couldn't endure one more spasm of sensation. "Oh," she cried out, "oh."

"That's right," he whispered, "go ahead, shout." His voice was rich with tenderness. She arched backward. His mouth was on her breast sucking, his fingers stroking deep, deep. The stream at their feet swelled to a roaring.

"Oh god," she cried. The stars were diamond points piercing. The river of sensation mounted to its final swell, running up, up, deep into her belly, melting her loins, shooting through her wave after wave. Every part of her was overcome, her shoulders, her arms, her throat, her eyes.

As the waves subsided, she choked up with love. She fell on him, burying her face in his loins, stroking her cheeks with his cock, pressing it to her neck, sucking the tip, running her tongue down the fine membrane of the underside.

"I knew it would be like this," she said, fiercely.

He propped himself on his elbows and watched her suck him, his eyes open wide. She licked the joints of his inner thighs, stroking his balls. The grass was velvety under her hips. She moved her face in deep, seeking the dark center where his cock emerged from his loin. Her lips traced a path around his balls. He watched with wired eyes. Then he was in her mouth again full.

He was divine. She couldn't show her adoration enough. Her hands stroked him everywhere, his pelvis, his balls, his thighs. Her throat wasn't nearly deep enough to take him in the way she longed to.

Again he stopped her, this time pulling her beneath him, parting her legs and thrusting in. She'd never been more open, more succulent with the sweet juices of her sex.

He stopped, withdrew quickly, fell down on her hungrily, his tongue sucking up the liquid. "I had to taste you again," he said, slipping his cock between her legs, pushing in deep, deeper, until the full shank stopped up everywhere it touched, until they were one man and woman wholly joined, born by the black and moving waters, into a lightless inner space where there was no time, only the eternity of their union. Again the mounting bliss...the apex...transformation...the rush of unleashed love.

Their union so complete, so profound was to come back to her in a cosmic image that sustained her in the years they were apart. In a half dream she saw her vulva as a lotus, its petals opened full. From its center a mushroom cloud rose up, the fiery pinnacles drawn down into the flower's center, dissolving into a perfect peace, a perfect harmony.

Tryst

Olga Broumas

The human cunt, like the eye, dilates
with pleasure. And all that joy never named

now arc priceless in the magnitude of the stars.
From are to are, have to have, beat subeternal.

By day, I found these on the beach, for you each
day and give. By night, remind me, I have

forgotten. Action replied by action, peace by peace.
Take you in all light and lull you on a sea

of flowers whose petals have mouths, mesmerized
centerfold, upsweep toward sleep.

Privacy

Olga Broumas

Finally
the only one I want
    to caress is you

You watch the changing
light across the sky
    I watch your eyes

Long Distance

Rita Speicher

By noon it's too hot to walk barefoot on the beach stones. I wear my thongs to take the six steps from my towel to water's edge, carrying a blue float, nothing like the blue of the water which today is green. I drift far from shore, but can still see the white house, the balcony with the clothesline Vera's now filling. Most of our clothes are white though I have a coral sun dress more popular than I imagined. When we bought my beach towel in the village we travel to once a week for food, I had a choice of green or orange. Vera chose green for me. I stood close to her holding the money. She asked how much and I thought I understood the merchant so I had the blue bills out of my pocket. This is one of her countries. Having never travelled, I compare it only to my own. "How far?" I asked before we left, meaning the distance between our village and the one with supplies. We had planned to start early that morning but by the time we finished breakfast and made it to the car the sun was whitening toward noon, the blue sky perfected like an act of simple charity. We parked on a narrow side street and walked to the main thoroughfare where Vera didn't notice men at tavernas follow her glide and profile. Vera's adventurous by inclination, not design, and if I had asked, we might never have made it back to the States. The street was animated by outdoor stands crowded with fruit, fabric, shoes, unfamiliar herbs. We felt each native peach before handing bags of them to the owner who approximated the weight. We bought fresh yogurt. I sat at an outdoor table, back to back with a priest in the full cloak of orthodoxy, watching Vera's hips cross the patio with my drink. After lunch we bought my towel and fresh butter cookies filled with apricot jam. Driving back, she nibbled at a spinach pie, balancing it on her knee between bites, licking her fingers. We sang a few songs and fiddled with the radio. From time to time we looked at each other, surprised, absorbed. We had opened all the windows; dry breeze collected in back like a passenger. We yawned and held hands till the road curved again. Without translation I understood the political slogans painted on the mountains claiming victory for right wing and left wing. We passed one hitchhiker, smoldering in afternoon heat, a wet bandana over her face like an outlaw. Once a red convertible passed, speeding in the other direction. Unloading the groceries, Vera asked "Should we have picked her up?" and I, having forgotten, smiled at the endurance of her thought; preoccupied with a piece of music, hours might pass between a question and its answer. Vera would score her first libretto in the fall, a cabaret.

The beach is empty except for my towel. And my thongs at the shoreline now nudged by the tide. I've been on the float longer than I expected, watching Vera hang laundry, then play a variety of instruments I can't hear from this distance — flute, dulcimer, sax — but recognize from the posture of her body. I paddle the float in a little circle, looking up: house, mountain, cloudless blue. Close to the peak everything is sanctified. When I rock, cool water trickles over the edge and I dam it between my thighs. Vera goes inside; first she waves, stands, turns. My thongs have drifted out, a few yards right, walking on water like an abandoned circus act. I slide in, tug the float with me. I haven't swam in water this clean since adolescence.

Heat radiates from the stones. The villagers don't come to the beach till six, after naps. I can actually see the heat waves, and the longer I watch the dizzier I become. A few times, a young girl brought an old woman in traditional black and buried her under the stones except for her head and once a big toe that she looked at instead of the horizon. It's difficult to imagine grief on this coast; the common air suckled and amorous with slow, crazed heat. You dive into the day; it parts and swallows you. You become familiar with possibility, as with an unrestrained woman. Even in the house, even napping on the cot, you're perched in the element.

I've written postcards and perused science magazines. I've waited. Friends arrived. At dinner we tell funny stories — or those gouged with destiny and sex. Night after night on the balcony of the same mountain restaurant we look down to the sea and up to the constellations, eating our salad, smoking our cigaret as if everything were usual or permanent or belonged to a constant benefactor. When I don't sit next to Vera, I sit across from her. When the table is round, I blush into the expanse. To the villagers — Vera translates — we are the "five girls alone." In the house, I'm crowded from her.

I follow dizziness into the exhaustion of waking, heavy-limbed, on my towel, the contour of my smell like a drawing into which I unwittingly release the transmigratory and aloof sex code of telepathy. I want to swim and eat peaches. I want to lie down with Vera. I want to bake us on the stones with the slow drug of the sun. Vera's strolling down the beach. Straw hat, Walkman, black bikini. She's in no hurry, and smiles. When she lies next to me, we chat and harvest tiny shells. Vera salvages all the blushed ones from my pile, offering in exchange the white and purple she collected.

One by one I take them, then lick the salt from the bowl of her palm. Each small act caresses the unspeakable with diversion — like the magician's. We are talking about adolescent sex. I tell Vera a story she likes. I'm thirteen and it's a very hot night. I'm at my parents' summer bungalow colony. The owners open the pool for a midnight swim. The caretaker's son is blond and muscular. We swim together. Short laps of the width at deep end. When I rest against the edge, he finds my hands underwater. He is fifteen and treading without effort. He smiles his blue eyes. We swim in a little circle, holding hands. I'm laughing. He has a name like Buddy or Skipper. We're surrounded by adults and splashing peers. He takes my hand underwater and grazes his crotch with it. His eyes give nothing of accident or intent. I blush. Again my hand is near his crotch. He opens my palm and presses it to him. I look away, wave to friends with my free hand. He rubs my palm against him. I feel him pulse. Instantly I pull away, kick off and swim to the other side of the pool. Someone connects the radio to the loudspeaker. The Platters are singing "My Prayer" and at the shallow end a bunch of boys mimic the lyrics and dunk each other. At deep end other teenagers are hiding in the shadows under the diving boards, holding on to floats and forbidden anatomy while our parents' voices rise, compete and finally coalesce to warn us not to stay in too long. Buddy or Skipper is swimming across to me, underwater. He surfaces slowly against my body, dragging his hands up the side of my thighs, over my hips, up my torso, links them under my arms, his thumbs grazing the top of my one-piece, lifts me away from the edge of the pool, and drops me so I sink and surface, targeting his face with a fine spray from between my teeth. He dives under again. This time when he surfaces he drags his hands up the inside of my thighs. He rests one finger against my crotch. An immediate warmth collects and spreads to my thighs, into the cool water, as if a dye; I look to see who notices. Our parents are beginning to leave or huddle around the card tables in the dark. The eighteen year olds are drifting through the gate to the other side of the bushes. My crowd is still in the water, howling, diving, hiding. His finger circles then taps then wanders to the elastic. He pulls on the band so water rushes in. His finger retreats and my hips thrust to follow. Two fingers on me now, pushing and circling. I come right away but he doesn't know and continues. He pulls at the elastic again and gets his whole hand in my suit. I wiggle against his palm. I'm wet different from the water. He slips one finger right up me and rubs my clit with his thumb. It feels like my heart needs to breathe. I try not to look in the direction of anybody, arching my neck to the stars, then come again. I do a back flip, stroke to the ladder, wave to him and get out.

It's Vera's turn. She tells the one about her cousin who was not really her cousin. Then we wash a peach and remain at water's edge. Vera inhales her food. We walk the float into the water, hold on with our arms and kick, sometimes tangling at the ankles. When we're out far enough to drift, Vera jumps on, unties the top of her bikini and covers her face with it. I ride her around for a while, changing her view from mountain to village to water and sun. "Splash me a little," she mumbles through her bikini top. I drip water between her breasts. It snuggles down to the slight rise of her belly, mixing with sweat. Vera has toned, smooth abdominals, creamy olive skin. "More," she sighs. I hold on to the float with my elbows, cup water in my hands and scoop it on to her chest. She massages the cool into her breasts and shoulders. "God, it's hot," she sighs. I pull down on the float, letting a little water over the edge. She wiggles it under her back and ass. I pull again. Willingly, she slides off, sinks under, her hair billowing on the water's surface like a sea flower come to life, while underwater her tongue grazes my collarbone. I wait for these moments like orbited astronauts must wait for God. We float on our backs, arms stretched, fingers twined—then Vera's behind me, palms under my shoulder blades, offering me, a memento, to the sky. She glides me back to the float and when I pull my body out of the swoon of water I see her friends waving from the beach. They drop their towels like warnings next to ours, amble to the shore, wade to mid-calf. Their eyes fix on us as if we're the lone attraction in this recluse beauty. Two are the color of instant cocoa, the other praline. I help Vera onto the float. We wobble and grab for each other. I clutch her elbow just as she catches the front of my bathing suit and we slide in opposite directions, Vera's torso over the side pulling my suit to my waist. Watched, we're both naked in their eyes now.

Some days Vera disappears through entire changes of light. Compelled, the rest of us enter an uneasy alliance. We brood. A motion at once solemn and hysterical collects us. Dance, it commands, and in the living room behind shades drawn against the broiling sun we turn into raucous athletic punks capable of a bitterness we mistake for irreverence. Talk, it insists, and lying on our bellies we do as the stone balcony cools through dusk and the sentimental charms us with its small, inaccurate mysteries. All gone as soon as Vera returns, humming or occupied, and each of us feigning indifference shifts our unobstructed loyalty to the frustration we know as desire. I always want to kiss Vera; face it, I tell myself, delighted by the transparent. If seen from the outside, I would think us fictitious and funny. I would want to join us. I travelled here because Vera invited me, and, if I was to follow the instinct connecting that bid to the future, witnessed literally like an image on a video screen, I had no choice but to arrive ready for the unconventional. It wasn't only a matter of faith. It was an opportunity to engrave the erotic with conscience.

Vera and I haul the float toward shore, Vera on her back lightly kicking. Deliberately, I'm the guide. I zigzag and waver. In the flat sea, I find corners to turn. I stall and lurch. If Vera said about face and head for the horizon, I'd obey. I'd marry her in this bathing suit. Naked I'd marry her, with or without brunch. Vera says nothing and I don't imagine she is waiting for me to say it. I surrender to the current. It lands us on the white lip of foam, ankle deep, where Vera's companions have waited. "Don't go," Vera whispers, so low I'm not certain I've heard it. I turn to her for confirmation. She's floating face down. She lifts her head. "C'mon," she says. Now the five of us maneuver the float — comic, indolent — jerking us into deep water where finally we loll as if our comfort were always this casual. The sun bakes our heads. Mild current lifts and drops us. I hallucinate a foot between my knees, climbing like an infidel toward the consecrated, till a sweep of toes across my crotch slams me against the real. I open my eyes. Vera's head is thrown back to the water and up to the sun, eyes closed, a smile, immodest and satisfied.

Before dinner I shower and lie out on the balcony. In the yard three white goats squat next to our white car. Scatchy tunes on the hi-fi from the house behind the bushes unravel into dusk. The sun strays in back of the mountain. I sing along with the best of the Everly Brothers — "All I Have To Do Is Dream," "Wake Up Little Susie." Sometimes Vera is slow; she shifts her weight from one foot to the other and an afternoon goes by. Other times quick, like now, brusque, transient thrill of lightening. She's wearing a peach halter, white skirt, and wants to borrow a sweater. We're the same height; once when measured back to back we remained attached long after the calculating hand withdrew, breathing together as though dancing. I'd like to ask Vera, was that your foot? was that permission swaddled in accident? is it time to kiss?

Later, the night flowers' thick scent will loosen us

like the wine we forget to buy, and straddling both it and Vera's fragrance I'll prepare the balcony with blankets. I sit across from Vera, patient as destiny in whose cult I am stripped. I want to rouse the hidden from its fancy shaft. I want Vera to play me with her lips, like the sax of stars. Spread on the blankets now, shoulder to shoulder. As the stars begin to dive in the flamboyant arcs of meteor shower, I reach for Vera, twining her to me as if our clasped hands cradled a vow, and all my attention — vivid, mindful of a persuasion that donates the sexual — takes her to the spasm of surprised delight, the orgasm public and yielded from which she cries mine.

Apples

Terry Lawhead

When my friend and I climb apple trees we go straight for the top where the best apples are. She clings to my pants and I cling to hers, I pull on her arms and she pulls on mine.

I've hung onto her belt when my feet have slipped and she holds firm to the tree trunk like a monkey. I would have probably died if she hadn't been there to hold me. I would have broken bones if she hadn't caught me with her legs. Once she scissored me around my chest with her legs, preventing a short fall, but I kept slipping down, nothing below me, my face buried in her stomach, my feet kicking in space. Her body is hard and sleek as a shark; she can move sideways and up and down and toward me and away, arching, as if she were in water. I pulled myself up by her own shoulders and pushed her down until she fell over backward from my weight, falling into the crotch of the limbs where they fold into the trunk of the tree. She smiled and offered herself to me. We loved each other with our pants around our ankles, soft flannel shirts open so lips could touch nipples and I could slip my hands around her small, round shoulders. I stuffed my jacket under her rump, keeping my elbows out to steady us as I held on to the smooth bark of new branches, balanced on a thick limb like swimming through the sea of the tree. Birds called out around us—I swear one landed on my head for a moment, I remember its wings and its tiny claws on my scalp. I think my friend held the bird, too, for a moment, with her hands invisible around my back, but I didn't ask her, everything was moving quickly and she was telling me about what the sky looked like through my hair, which fell across her eyes, how she always wanted my hair to lie across her eyes and I was too happy to notice anything but how she kept opening beneath me.

We almost fell off, rolling like a bottle in the sea in that tree. But we rolled into another embrace of tree limbs, putting me on the bottom and her on the top, and she reached up to keep climbing, leaving me to watch her with the blue sky and sunlight above her, her rump shining like the biggest loveliest apple of all. We let our pants fall away and kept climbing barefoot and half-naked, going for the top, for the best apples up high in the best light. I liked coming from beneath her and entering her that way. She is as strong as I am and would brace herself hanging from the limbs while I would go inside of her fast, dangling like an opossum from her back. If she had let go we both would have died. Nobody wants to die, we only want love, and to feel good outside in the fresh air, and to hear birds singing when our own hearts are bursting. She never let go. We kept climbing, to the top where the best apples are, where the light is best.

There are many apples up high, but nobody else ever tries to get them. There are smaller limbs up there, sleek and flexible, and I stand on them with her, her legs wrapped around me, her chin on my shoulder as she takes me again and again, rising and falling, arching up and backward like tall waves, like the tree limbs in night winds. The limbs bend way down when I move inside of her, the new young tips whip in the air. Young, slender limbs never break, they only yield, they accept everything without breaking, and we move however we want knowing we are safe. We look up into the sun together and move as fast as we can, not knowing if now we are falling, turning slowly in the air toward the ground where we could die broken inside of each other. Birds circle the tree singing, watching to see if we can make it to the top, where the best apples are. I stand behind her holding her breasts which are like the best apples and we can see far over the other treetops and fields, we are higher than anybody else has ever been; only the clouds are higher, and they lying together, fold open and closed to rising warmth like shells in the sea. We are all of us, clouds and people and seeds within apples living on this earth like the hermits of shells in the sea.

But we can still go higher, and her breasts fill my hands as she bends to hold me for a moment, large and red and glistening in the bright air, and put me back inside of her, slippery and eager, and she crouches and stands and sucks me and rolls me, again and again, her thighs white as the fruit of apples. I lick her neck and it tastes like apples, and I hold her head in my hands; now nothing keeps us on the limb but our own balance and how the tree opens to the wind, we are depending upon the invisible opening and closing of the limbs, like hands weaving a basket, to keep us up. And I pray with her head in my hands as she wiggles within small doughnuts and I feel again we must be falling now to our deaths together. I pray that we will grow old together and wake up every morning in each others arms and see the sky together before anybody else is out on the street. I want to always be just outside of her in the cool air, where I feel my own body and know I must accomplish this climb alone, but ready to plunge deeply into her warm sea again and hear her breathing on my cheek, willing to open again and again for me. We are barely balanced on the tallest slenderest limbs, her feet are set like a ballet dancer slightly pointed outward, her arms are out in the

air, her spread fingers are barely touching other small
limbs touching back. It is like being on a peninsula in
the sky, only I am able to move inside of her and feel her
ribs and breasts and round shoulders with my hands.
We are held there by a thousand small fingers balancing
us, introducing us to the audience of the sky. I love her
shoulders when I hold her from behind, they are like
small firm apples pressed against my cheek. It is possible
to pull overselves up over one another to reach the next
highest limbs, she climbs over me clinging to me, her
fingers in my mouth and I hold my tongue between her
thumb and fingers. We suddenly slip, it happens so
quickly I think she is no longer with me, that we have
lost each other forever, and that I will never truly see
anything peacefully again, but that the rest of my life
will be a series of collisions and pain, but I have only
dropped a foot. I push my face into the warm wet center
of her body to hold her up so she can reach the next limb
and hang on while we rest. She opens more so I can enter
more, I leap in deeper than I have ever been and see
another world I have never known, the world of blood
and juice longing for fullness and ripeness and there are
blossoms of every fruit desiring penetration and eter-
nities of stillness. I push her up with my tongue, I can
hold her in that apple tree with my tongue, she lets go of
the limb and I turn on my limb and she is balanced on
my tongue. Birds come land on her outstretched hands,
I point my tongue straight up and she drops down two
inches onto my face, and the birds flutter in her hands
and she cries out in joy. As she lifts off she clenches and
pulls me up behind her, I hold onto her thighs and she
pulls me right up, we rise toward the best apples at the
top where the light is best. The top of the tree has barely
any limbs at all, they disappear into the light, going
higher where we cannot see. Birds disappear into those
upper branches, our own future as old people is up there
invisible. These little twigs bend even when a bird lands,

but the apples are huge and shiny and everywhere; these are the apples nobody can see from the ground, they are the apples everybody is longing for on the ground but cannot see and don't dare to climb up to find. They glisten like old Christmas ornaments, they are more protective than all of the royalty of Africa, more sacred than the bright bells of Tibet. My friend takes off her flannel shirt and now is completely naked and shiny among the red apples, and I rub the apples on her body, over her breasts and stomach and thighs, and she smiles and shivers and embraces me. The apples are everywhere around us, the light is bright and warm. Our red skin reflects the apples, she falls back into a weave of branches full of apples and raises her legs, balanced perfectly as she straddles all the apples and rocks back and forth, picking them up in her hands and back of her knees and the inside of her elbows and one big one in her mouth. She chews and swallows bits of apple while her eyes laugh and her long hair flows out over the apples and I lie across her so that our bodies cross. We stretch out and lie quietly in the bed of apples and soft leaves and sunlight, the branches sway under our weight. We may be falling now in our net of ripe apples, or we may be floating away on our raft of ripe apples, and she holds me to guide me inside of her and I turn back; like the hands of a human clock we turn back to face one another at this moment at the top of the tree where the biggest apples are, and below her are apples and blue sky and the green depths of leaves and green fields. Cool apples push up against my thighs, against my warm body. She rises up against me, birds soar around us, singing, we are up at the highest limbs in the sunlight of our bodies, where the best apples are.

Snow Climbers

Steve Wiesinger

we touch fingertips
climb feet against feet
toward Sierra peaks
where the air leaps
catch our breath that flies away
with rising birds
and then follow the crevice
where your flesh turns
a long line inward
clear to the small of your back
I move carefully
as a snow climber
near red mountain flowers
while you lead with hips
certain and gentle as a hand

Fish

Charlotte Mendez

Her beloved hesitated a moment just as she was near the tumbling waterfall, the cataract. He thought, perhaps, that she had already gone over, while she in turn hoped that he would keep the torrent roiling just that moment longer, that she might be flung far, far, farther than ever before in the glittering, foaming waters. In that moment of hesitation she felt their separateness, she felt the sadness, she felt the lowering of water tables throughout the world.

But before she could murmur a word to him, before he could tenderly inquire of her, a great fish leapt out of the waters and swooped down upon them. She saw the forward-placed silver-rainbow eyes rush toward her, the pink mouth open swiftly and scoop her into it. Down she slipped into the rosy chamber, where she fit just snugly, the momentum pushing her arms against her naked sides. Since the fish had swallowed her headfirst, she was traveling feet first now, at great speed. She wondered briefly if this might be some new kind of coming — a sort of going — but the speeding fish was too purposeful, like a very fast commuter train as it carried her along; there was no sense of abandon, of rapture — though perhaps a little feeling of rescue. But if the fish swam purposefully, they must have some destination. Bits of foam were refreshing the soles of her feet, tapping at them in little irregular bursts, or plashes.

Some destination. A quiet pool in which to digest her perhaps? Strangely, the thought didn't trouble her; such discomfort seemed remote. For now she enjoyed the speed and the flow. After all, only moments ago she had felt waters receding all over the planet, had felt herself about to be beached, apologetic, lonely, next to her beloved.

Was he frantic? Had he rushed to call the rescue boats? Or had he not yet noticed her absence, was he sleeping peacefully?

She opened her eyes. It was not all darkness within, as she'd expected. The fish seemed to be made of glass, of deep blue and soft nasturtium colors, flowing into one another. Through its translucent sides she could see bubbles and waves rushing past, could glimpse the shadowy forms of other fishes.

These looked in at the naked form of a woman, arms at her sides, toes tipped upwards while her feet caught the inflowing spray, her body's undulations more intricately elaborating the curves of the fish. Her tender surfaces caressed by the withinness of the fish, her own soft nasturtium colors echoing the color of the fish's sides, its blue fins keeping them both in the spirit, the colors, of the waters.

Becoming part of the fish in some way—perhaps its prisoner, perhaps its luxuriant passenger, perhaps itself, perhaps its lover—she lay in bewilderment in the midst of the colors and speed. Did she not have fins? Did the fish not have arms?

It grew darker. They entered a violet, indigo-violet deep sea twilight. Silver glints still indicated bubbles swirling past them. But it grew too dark for the shadows of other creatures to be seen where she lay. A slowing now, deep into the violet. No more glints of silver. They hung in the dark clear waters, in the indigo half-light, the silence. The mouth of the fish had shut firmly long minutes ago. Its sides seemed to press in against her, to push at her, so that suddenly the bright foaminess of the air was gone. She could barely breathe, and yet she did not panic. Her breath simply suspended in the silence.

There was an unexpected bliss in being so pressed in upon from all sides. She relaxed into it and felt herself going forth into some rapture of closeness, of being held, of being loved sufficiently and wholly. The pressure squeezed up her thighs and over her belly, pushed down on her breasts and in at her waist and the small of her back, oh so deliciously! and moved in a wave up her shoulders, down her arms, around her face, into her hair even, electrifying it. And then back again, the wave began at the soles of her feet, a little slap, and then a push and warm against her knees, her thighs again, and she found herself oh yes, most exquisitely coming, that rapture spreading everywhere now, the bursting forth, the bursting through!

Suddenly she was free. Her neck rolled back in the dark waters, her wet hair dragging and cooling her scalp. She spun over onto her belly; her legs, her arms reaching out freely. Still in rapture, still in abandon she floated.

The fish, her mother, swam round and came back to her while still aimlessly she floated in the water, trying her arms a bit, breathing from somewhere within, she knew not how. The fish came around again, sliding its belly across the small of her back, then nudging and spinning her slowly about. She reached out both palms to caress the fish as it glided over her once and yet again it came by, and softly the woman reached out her hand and felt the great side of the fish slide along her palm caressingly, to the final tickle of the crisp tail fin. Come, it seemed to say as it flicked against her palm, and like a baby dolphin she began to swim after, her arms flung forward, her feet fluttering.

What will it be, this new life I am in? She remembered her beloved, whom she had never even known, who had never known her. Did he remember her? Was he still sleeping?

She remembered the desire which had brought them together, the rich consciousness of one another in which they had basked and hungered and fed. How rich and thrilling it had been then; how dry and frictive compared to this. She was swimming now in a brighter part of the ocean. Others swam by her now, some swiftly, some more slowly. Their silent, active presence filled her with a new desire. She longed to be back inside the fish that she might be enclosed in that glassy blue and nasturtium coloring, worthy of the magentas, the scarlets, the silvers, that flashed around her. But the great fish was gone. And she in her pale skin had no ornament but the curving of her body's form, the moderate fling and spreading of her hair. Oh form, what is it you contain? she asked each shape which came to her. She asked that variety of fins, filmy and wavy and many-colored, stiff and pleated and translucent; that variety of eyes on stalks and eyes placed here and there alluringly, and mouths of sweetly various erotic forms. There was no answer, but only the continued invitation to dance among them, gliding near and passing, then passing again as the small bubbles rose in straight lines, and all else was undulant and silent and constantly changing.

Sexy

M.M. Roberts

Once I was driving through North Idaho with my girlfriend and we started talking sexy. She didn't know what "tumescent" meant. She wasn't kidding. I told her. She liked it. We discussed "erectile" and catalogued its geography. She smiled. I suggested we turn off the highway for awhile. She concurred and sat a bit forward in her seat. The first few turnoffs had campers or other distractions, then we found one unoccupied. We drove a mile or so into the piney woods to a small white bridge over a creek so shallow it couldn't drown an ankle. We parked. I got the car blanket out of the back. We walked downstream. Soon we found a meadow just a few inches higher than the creek and just big enough for us. I spread the blanket. It was very small but so was the creek. We undressed and I placed my shirt and pants at the edge of the blanket to make it bigger. We lay down. We kissed on one another. We rolled around. We made noises. We crushed some grass and leaf. The sun. The woods. She smiled. We kissed. Later she got up and squatted in the creek, dabbing at her thighs and sweet union with handfuls of sparkling water. It was the loveliest thing I've ever seen.

Sand Angel

Joy Passanante

For my birthday, a nondescript Monday in May, Ginny gave me binoculars. Since I was neither a hunter nor a birdwatcher, I thought at the time this was a strange gift, indeed. For her birthday a few weeks later I gave her perfume, a scent the lady with the beehive hairdo in David's Department Store recommended, and considered the matter closed.

The next day we left for the Selway. For six days I faithfully swept out the tent, stacked wood for fires, gazed at constellation after constellation, and zipped our musty-smelling sleeping bags together, waiting for the Selway to take us into its heart — in the charade that a week in the wilds could resurrect us. On the seventh day I dutifully woke up to make the fire and boil water for coffee. I opened the food chest and lifted the can. It was so light I shook it, then snapped open the plastic lid and hurled the empty can at the tent. I grabbed my binoculars and stomped a step or two toward the trail, then took a deep breath and glanced behind me. At the door to the tent Ginny stood in slumped profile, hands heavy at her sides. Sweat stained a sloppy circle under her armpit. Her blue jeans bulged with the bulk of her hip.

Kicking the charred remains of last night's campfire, I pulled my shirt over my head, crumpled it into a ball, and threw it back. I didn't wait to see where it landed.

For a week the air had been uncomfortable even at night. And my inner heat had been rising.

I angled up the gently curving trail with oversized strides, steaming inside, snapping twigs under my boots. The path wound along boulders and the fat double-ranked needles of Grand fir flapped against my shoulder on the left as I trudged on, once in a while glancing down below me on the right. At the foot of the steep slope a strip of white beach glittered as if the sand were dotted with diamonds. The river pooled blue-green; silvery fish wriggled, small waves fanning at the surface.

I caught her out of the corner of my eye in a kayak and stepped behind a boulder. She paddled to shore. As she stepped out, she glanced up the bank toward the path, and me, and scanned the trail, one side, then the other. No breeze gave me away; the dust was still, unclouded.

From behind the boulder, spruce needles scraped my face. My gaze riveted on the girl on the beach, but I refused to take the binoculars out of my pack. In a white two-piece swimsuit tied in bows mid-back and at the hips, she faced the river. Her hair was titian thread-ed with gold and seemed untamable as a forest fire. Even though it was clipped at the neck, tiny tendrils escaped around her head and the blond tips of each hair held the light around it like a halo. She removed the clip and the hair fell to the base of her spine. For a moment I was startled by a rustling—a squirrel or a chipmunk, perhaps—in the brush behind me, and when I focused again on the woman, she was naked.

I grabbed the binoculars.

Her tan lines, which gave her a dual quality, sug-gested that she was a novice at nudity. She knelt on the sand and bent toward the pool, her buttocks rounded and tipped up toward me, ivory below the brown line which drew a horizon from hip to hip. She cupped her hands into the water and lifted them to her mouth, water spilling in rivulets onto her forearms. That particular pose triggered a flushed heat, and I drew from my pocket my red bandanna to tie it around my head. I wanted to cup my hands around those fleshy crescents, remove the bandanna, and blot the glistening beads of July heat which ran down between her shoulder blades and pooled at the indentations at the base of her back — as if some deity in an immortal act of love had pressed both thumbs first into the small of her back, then farther down to form twin dimples on those dual milky crests.

She waded into the river and walked upstream with her profile to me, hands cupped over her breasts as if to prolong their protection from the full shock of the freezing stream. I imagined the sting of the icy pool on naked flesh, radiating from the core and instantly quickening every nerve.

Onshore again, she gathered up her hair and wound it behind her neck and over a shoulder, then lay back and wiggled a bit to press her body firmly into the sand. In a deft movement she opened her legs. I drew in a sharp breath. Then she raised her arms, imprinting the sand with triangles just a slight shade darker than the hitherto undisturbed white surface. I might have sworn she was doing jumping-jacks on the wrong plane, a horizontal, grounded one. Then I realized she was making a snow angel on the virgin sand.

I christened her Angel, and as I was musing over the angel-shape on the sand, a yellow-jacket wasp spiraled down from the cloudless sky. At first, without opening her eyes, she waved it away. It circled back and flew in crazy-eights above her face. She opened one eye and watched it. I raised my lens to examine her companion. Its body was long, taut, trembling, striped with the colors of summer on the Selway — the dark of the shade from the Engleman spruce, the yellow heart of the uncompromised sun — and promising the sting of the icy water. I imagined the power of that cold current, concentrated in a poisoned puncture, single and minute.

Suddenly the insect swooped down, bisecting the triangle her open legs formed in the sand, turned and soared up to orbit her right nipple, which seemed to jut up as if excited, then her left nipple, which also rose and hardened. As it alighted on the patch of copper-colored hair between her legs, my arm jerked and I watched in horror as my binoculars rolled down the embankment and bounced off a moss-coated boulder, landing where the woods became beach.

My pulse froze as she sat up at the sound of falling rock and loosened dirt, her legs still spread, and I dropped to the dirt behind a tree. She leaned on her arms and, as if in an unconscious act of modesty, divided her hair at the back, quickly drew half over each breast, and searched for the source of the noise.

The choice was clear: I could scramble down the embankment and utter something asinine like, "Oh, don't mind me; I'm just looking for my opera glasses." Or, I could remain snake-like in the dust, the spruce needles pressing lines into my face and my chest smelling like sap, perhaps for the rest of my life.

Or, I could wait until Angel lay back and closed her milky-white eyelids against the sun and sprint back to camp, cowering from spruce to fir like some cartoon culprit — and return to Ginny without my binoculars. The image of Ginny watching me unwrap the silver paper and shiny bow, her expectant half-smile affording me ample view of the space between her front teeth, gave me a chill.

"Hey, buddy."

My stomach lurched. I'm hallucinating, I told myself.

"Hey, buddy. It's all right. Go get your glasses. I know you're dying to."

The accent was New Jersey—Hoboken, or Hackensack, but definitely New Jersey.

"Sorry," I heard myself mumbling. Then when there was silence, I yelled, "Sorry!"

"No prob."

Why are we having this inane conversation? I thought, briskly pulling myself up onto my arms, then squatting as if this were the only natural stance one could take after emerging from hiding prone in the dirt. I brushed myself off nonchalantly and picked off a "V" of pine needles which stubbornly remained stuck with sap to my chest like some parody of a corsage. I was tempted to grab the glasses and flee, but something made me brazen it out. When I looked her square in the face, I saw that she was smiling.

"How long were you peeping?"

The word "peeping" kindled my anger, though perhaps it was sparks of shame that ignited it. Trying to pretend ignorance of the awkwardness of the situation, I strode as deliberately as I could down the hill to the edge of the beach, picked up the glasses, and wiped the lenses on the side of my jeans.

As I pivoted to leave, she said, "Well? Are you gonna sunbathe or not?"

At first I hesitated. Then I turned to steal a glance. She was spread-eagled and a pool of perspiration had collected between her breasts and in her belly button. I wondered if the insides of her thighs were also damp, but I was afraid to look at that soft triangle of hair too long.

I placed my binoculars on a flat rock close to her feet, then knelt and with all the aplomb I could summon lay down parallel to her, the sand burning my chest a little. I hoped it muted the sound of my heart thudding against it. My arms were at my sides, my hand an inch or so, about the length of the yellowjacket away, from hers. I tried to concentrate on her hand, naked except for a silver snake ring set with a turquoise eye, so that I wouldn't stare at her curves. I squirmed a bit in the sand, my hips burrowing in to adjust myself in my jeans. I thought since she seemed to have her eyes closed, she wouldn't notice, but she must have heard something or felt some vibrations, because without turning her head, her eyes still tight against the sun, she grinned. And before I could respond, make some excuse, before my gaze could dart back to her hand, she rolled over in one graceful motion onto my back.

For three or four minutes she just rested there; I could feel her heart push steadily against my shoulder blade. Once I absorbed that feeling, accepted it into my continually revised sense of what is natural and logical, I felt those two taut nipples like velvet-covered nail-heads press firmly into my skin. I pressed my pelvis farther into the sand and raised my rear to meet her body. She slowly lay her arms over mine and rested her head in the bend of my neck. Her thick hair over my face made me think of a forest of flames. It distracted me from her weight and her heat and my own breathing. I was half afraid the river would carry that sound, the only human sound in the Selway.

Escapist that I am, I might have lost myself in this contemplation, but after sound penetrated my consciousness I realized there was also movement, and I felt the gentle circling of her pelvis on my behind. Round and round she led in a rhythm that might have been mesmerizing had I been watching instead of feeling its effects. It took only a second or two before I realized she was merely mocking my own gauche little pelvic dance in the sand of a few minutes earlier. In another context I might have been furious, but her relentless rhythm, those naked breasts against my back, and our lower bodies just a piece of fabric apart were drowning out all impulses but the sensual, the immediate. A sudden and insistent urge to be front to front made me move my arms. As I raised them above my head, hers rode with them. Then I felt a steady pressure on both arms, and, as if she were leading in an odd dance of just the arms, they moved down to our sides again.

Our arms together made a full circle, bisected by our torsos, from over our heads to our sides. Then the legs. At first just a little nudge to spread them, then a driven rhythm — close, open, close, open — opening wider each time. Sand angels facing down. Sand angels in tandem. If the throbbing in my loins hadn't been surging to a dangerous peak, I might have laughed.

Suddenly I drew in my arms 'til they were tight at my sides, stiffened my thigh muscles so that my legs remained straight. Her body tensed; she drew in three long breaths and exhaled, then she relaxed.

I shifted slightly onto my side to turn us both so we were face to face. As if she sensed both my desire and my awkwardness, she smoothly rolled away and said, "C'mere," and took my hand, held it to that lily and primrose breast, then pulled me over her. I raised my body to position myself and was about to lower onto her, when she raised her palm and held it flat against my chest. My heart pounded madly, and my arm muscles trembled with my own weight and need. As I held myself parallel over her, she unbuttoned my jeans and with her thumbs slid them down my hips. She sat up a little to push them down to my knees, and the slight quiver in her breasts when she moved, and the feel of the hard nipples grazing my chest, shot adrenaline up and down my thighs. I pushed off my jeans.

Then she slipped her arm around my back. As she pressed her hand steadily down, I lowered myself, first hovering above her so I could feel her skin, but just barely, all the way down. From my toes up my legs to my pelvis, from the tips of my fingers down my arms into my chest, every muscle flooded with blood and readiness.

"Angel," I whispered, tasting the salt above her soft upper lip and straining to hold back. "Angel," I said more urgently; and still I paused at the precipice, to keep from plunging over it quite yet, to keep from ending it. But the sweet ascent was already beginning, and I knew I could hold off no longer. I could feel it rise from my thighs. I pressed my taut body onto hers and was about to sink into her as she whispered into my open mouth, "Not Angel, buddy. Virginia."

I felt as if I had been stung by a wasp. Virginia. Ginny. Virginia. Ginny. The greasy dishpan, the ripped pocket of the workshirt, its faded cross-stitching. As I struggled desperately, grinding against the body beneath me to try to force it to return me to the fiery realm where it had promised to deliver me, my foot, like a panicked fish on a hook, flailed out and struck something hard. We both stiffened at the sound of an object falling into water, and I knew it was too late. I didn't even have to turn around to see through the transparent pool the binoculars sinking towards bits of quartz speckling the dark sand of the riverbed, as if they belonged there. In my mind I saw them swept up by the current, battered in a vortex of froth, and hurled down uncharted falls, precipitous and deadly.

I stared at Angel's open, blue-green eyes and saw in them the river behind me.

They All Look Alike in the Dark

Susan Moon

"**Is** there anybody in here?" asked the man, stepping into the dark sauna. The heavy door—a door fit for a dungeon—groaned shut behind him, but there was no other answer. He stumbled over the rough planks of the floor to the benches, feeling in front of him with his hands. The adobe room was built right over a natural hot springs, and heated by the sulphurous steam that rose through cracks between the planks. It almost burned the soles of your feet if you stood still over one of these cracks. He couldn't see the bunch of herbs that had been hung from the ceiling—eucalyptus, sage, and mint—but he could smell them. "Whew! It's hot in here," he said out loud.

"Yes, isn't it?" said a woman's voice, then.

The man jumped. "Oh! You startled me! Why didn't you answer before?"

"I'm sorry," she said. "I guess I'm pretty spaced out."

"Where are you, anyway?" He sat cautiously on the first bench, lifting his feet from the burning floor. He was fairly sure from the direction of her voice that he wouldn't sit down on top of her.

"I'm up here on the top shelf, with the canned goods."

He stretched out on his back on the lower bench, where it wasn't quite so hot. A rock had been placed at the end of the bench to be used as a pillow, and he found it surprisingly comfortable. She had a nice voice. He reminded himself to breathe deeply, relax. He was here to relax. "It sure is dark and warm and wet in here," he said. "Does it remind you of a place you lived in for a while, long, long ago?"

"Well, it's a lot hotter in here than it was there." He was relieved that she understood his reference. "And besides," she went on, "I didn't have any company in there. But I'm glad to have your company—it was eerie to be in here alone in the dark."

"I can imagine. Like being inside of your own head, with no external reference points."

"Are you a therapist, too?" Her voice was teasing. "Everybody here seems to be some kind of therapist."

He thought there was a charming combination, in her talk, of skepticism and naivete. On the one hand she seemed quite willing to play a game of boy-meets-girl-at-sensitivity-workshop, and on the other hand she seemed to say what was on her mind, without artifice. "What makes you ask if I'm a therapist?"

"Now I *know* you're a therapist, answering a question with a question like that. You're a dead giveaway."

She was smart, too. "Well, O.K., you've gotta be a therapist yourself, or else in therapy. To know that."

"No, I'm neither one, believe it or not. I must have seen it in the movies, or something. But you know—I feel like a member of an endangered species; the unshrunk. Preserve our natural wildlife. Save the Unshrunk Now."

He thought she was shy, in spite of her talking. How strange it was to meet someone this way, as if blind. But blind people could at least reach out and touch each other, shake hands. This was stranger still because of their nakedness, which meant that they must take care not to touch. How embarrassing it would be, for example, if he reached up to shake her hand and grabbed her breast by mistake. She might think he did it on purpose.

But the sense of intimacy was marvelous. He had her voice, her sweating presence, in the emptiness. The utter darkness returned them both to their original nature. They were twins, unborn, unformed. She could be anyone, she *was* anyone, and he could imagine her as he chose. Behind her voice her female form shifted kaleidoscopically according to his fancy. He hoped no one else came into the sauna.

"Well, *are* you a therapist?" she pressed him.

"Yes, after a fashion."

"Which fashion?"

"You're a curious girl, aren't you?" No sooner had he said the word 'girl' then he regretted it. She was sure to be a feminist. Should he correct himself? "I believe in curiosity," he went on. "I'm a curious boy myself." That should take care of it, if it wasn't too transparent. "I'm not trying to put you off, by the way—I'm getting into body work, now. Very little verbal work anymore."

"I see," she said. He saw her as he wanted her, with his mind's eye: stretched out, long-legged, on the bench, hip bones erect, small-waisted, heart-shaped face, dark eyes and hair, dangling arm that pulled her breast to the side. He was getting hot; he wasn't going to last much longer.

"Do you come to these workshops often?" he asked her.

"I've been to several. It's how I like to take my vacations."

"What are you on vacation from, if I may ask?"

"You may. I'm an astrologer." There was a slight edge in her voice, that said she'd been ridiculed.

He was taken aback, fought off his assumption that all astrologers were starry-eyed hippies. She could be serious. "Far out," he said. She snorted. "No, really, I mean it." He tried to sound enthusiastic. "Do you actually make a living at it?"

She laughed. "I actually do. Not just doing charts for people, but I teach some classes, too."

"You must live in the Bay Area, if you can support yourself that way."

"Oh, no, L.A. That's where the real hard-line stargazers live, didn't you know? But I bet you live in the Bay Area, right?"

"Right. But I'm *not* going to tell you my sign," he teased.

"Maybe I know it already." He could almost hear her smiling. Again he wondered if her appearance was as pleasing as her voice. To match her speech, her gait should have a lilt, her head and shoulders a shy swagger.

He wanted to stay and talk longer, but his flesh was roasting, all soft and pink. "I'm fading fast," he said. "If I had an apple in my mouth, I'd be a roast suckling pig."

"Really? Are you plump?"

"You don't stand on ceremony, do you? No, I'm not plump, but I'm old enough to have to fight it off, I'll tell you that." He wanted to take the opportunity to ask her if *she* was plump, but he didn't dare venture on such dangerous ground. Women were more sensitive about that than men, and the truth was, he could see why. An overweight woman bothered him more than an overweight man. He knew it was for the wrong reasons, but he couldn't help it. He didn't want the voice to be fat. Among the people he'd seen arriving for the workshop that afternoon, he'd noticed two women who were quite attractive, though one of them had been on the heavy side. He hoped he hadn't seen his sauna mate at all, so far. He hoped that she had a long neck, a long body, that she was, in short, a gazelle. Her olive skin shone with sweat, or would, if there was light to shine by, or so he imagined. Tomorrow by daylight he'd find out which one she was, and in the meantime, the suspense was pleasurable.

He felt dizzy. He touched his own hot thighs. How spongy his skin felt! But while his body was completely enervated by the sauna, his mind bloomed with desire. "I hate to leave your company," he said, "but I've got to go before I completely evaporate." How could he secure something of their meeting for the future? He wanted to ask if she would be there again tomorrow night, but felt it would be pressing too hard. "Talk to you later," he said.

The following morning, Monday, they had the introductory meeting of the week-long workshop in perceptual consciousness. There was to be no talking during the workshop sessions, or during meals, as part of their awareness practice. He was assigned to the morning group, in which he noticed several women he thought were very attractive. Perhaps his sauna partner was one of them.

The two leaders worked as a team, and were able to demonstrate by silent example what they wanted the participants to do, whether it was slowly rotating a partner's leg at the hip joint, or walking around the room with a bean bag on your head, for these constituted the activities of the first meeting. His hip-rotating partner was another man, a colleague of his from San Francisco. As he lay on his back in a patch of sun, and his old friend kneeled beside him, pushed up the cloth of his pants to grasp his ankle, and slowly bent his leg at the knee, he tried to pay attention to the sensations at the hip, but a self-conscious laugh spluttered out: they never would have foreseen this moment when they were interns together.

The food was excellent. He ate more than he should have at lunch, especially of the walnut torte, and then he returned to his cabin. It would have been a pleasure to share his siesta with a female companion, but this was only the first day. There was still plenty of time for a shipboard romance. This rule of silence, though, made things difficult.

He lay on his bunk to read, but started to daydream instead, of how he might initiate a conversation with the redhead he'd noticed at lunch. Then he scolded himself for being so horny. He reminded himself that there was more to life than getting laid, that the workshop itself was enjoyable, that he was learning some body-work techniques that would be useful professional tools, that he was getting a much-needed rest in a beautiful spot.

On the other hand, he certainly didn't have to feel guilty for hoping that a sexual encounter would be part of this trip. He was a hard-working psychiatrist, divorced, loyal to his teenage children, and he took only two weeks vacation a year. Oh, but the midday heat was soporific, with the stream gurgling its lullaby past his cabin.

He must have been asleep for about an hour, when he woke up, sweaty and groggy. A swim would freshen him up, and then a bask on the hot boulders. He wandered down to the creek, and followed it downstream, through the woods, on a path that was dappled with shadows and lizards. Above the canyon in which he walked, the golden summer mountains loomed protectively, keeping out everything that was ugly, and on their slopes, by rocky outcroppings, the century plant sent forth its phallic bloom. The air smelled of sage. He came round a bend in the path to the place where a waterfall made a deep pool in the rocks, perfect for swimming. A good-looking woman lay spread out naked on a big rock, like a pat of butter melting on a pancake. Her eyes were closed, affording him the opportunity to stare unabashedly at her nakedness. Ah, nothing like the Growth Movement — good old California Hip. She was the redhead he'd noticed at lunch, freckled and bony, but with a luxuriance of pubic hair, even redder than the hair on her head. She could be the sauna girl, though he'd thought of her as a bigger woman. Was it only that he wished her so? Irritated at himself for having such a one-track mind, he resolved not to make any overtures to this sunbather, but to leave her in peace, and thereby regain some dignity in his own eyes.

When he came out of the trout-flecked water, tingling with the cold, to dry off on the rocks, the redhead was gone.

On Monday evening it was with considerable excitement, really more than the occasion warranted, he told himself, that he pushed open the heavy door of the sauna.

"Anybody home?" he asked. He was answered by more than one voice—it could have been two or three or four—and he couldn't tell whether the voice from last night was among them. Further questioning revealed that the middle bench was occupied by a strange man's voice and a strange woman's voice, a couple, no doubt, and that the bottom bench, where he sat down, was empty. There were no remarks from the top shelf. The middle voices were chatting about the workshop.

"I was just *amazed,*" said the female voice, "how I felt it in my whole body when that guy was moving my leg around."

"What guy? What guy?! said the male voice in mock jealousy. "If he tries that again I'll smash his teeth down his throat!"

He shuddered at the violent image.

Then the voice dropped its joking tone to say, "But I know what you mean. It even changed my breathing. I felt opened up, like my yin energies were really released."

If she was up there, she must have recognized his voice when he came in. Why wouldn't she speak her presence to him? He cleared his throat. "Is anybody up there with the canned goods?" he asked.

Except for somebody scratching something, there was an embarrassed silence.

"What did you say?" came middle female voice at

last, to dissipate the question.

"Never mind, I'm just sort of thinking out loud. You get so relaxed in here—"

"Damn right," said male middle voice. "But I think the food here is right on, don't you?"

The door opened. "Anybody in?" said the voice he'd been waiting for. Greetings were exchanged all around, and she climbed up to the top bench, without touching him. There ware more talk of food, which he did not engage in. He was concentrating all his efforts on keeping cool. He wanted to stay until the couple left, and talk alone with her. Damn them, anyway, they'd been in here before him; surely they were done to a turn by now. What a ridiculous situation.

"Do you find you get used to his heat the more you do it?" he asked. Yes, they all did. "Well, maybe I'll last a little longer tomorrow night, then," he said, to show he'd be there. "But for now, I sure have lost my cool." The groan that always follows a bad pun ushered him out the door.

Tuesday, in his morning session, he had a fat blonde woman for his partner. He'd noticed her before, because she had such enormous and sympathetic eyes. She lay on her back and when he slowly moved her arm in circles through the air, he couldn't help observing how the fat hung down from her upper arm, moving, to stay in plumb, as he moved her arm. When he, in his turn, lay down and closed his eyes, cool hands touched his forearm. Then his arm was raised with such delicacy that he lost the feel of her hands, and his arm seemed to levitate by magic, for his muscles were relaxed. As this arm of his moved through the air, in slow unanticipated arcs, he felt how well-made his shoulder joint was, how his shoulder blade responded, moving against the floor, how the yoke of his collarbone served to distribute the slightest stress, in fact, how well put together he was, and he felt in perfect harmony with the agent of this realization, even if she was fat.

Tuesday night he entered the sauna a little later than the night before, with the same question: "Anybody home?"

"Yes, me," said the voice, from its usual spot. He told her he'd been disappointed that they had had company the night before.

"Why? What did you have in mind?"

"Oh, just continuing our conversation." He asked her if she was enjoying the workshop sessions, and which group was she in, and she said yes, she was, and she was in the morning group. So she could be the fat blonde. He asked her if she'd been down to the swimming hole by the waterfall, and she said yes, wasn't it beautiful there? So she could be the redhead.

He said, "Where is everybody, anyway? I mean why are we usually the only ones in here?"

"Most people like the other saunas better," she said. "They're closer to the cold creek, so you can plop right into it."

"Well, then, why do *you* come in here?" he asked.

"Maybe in hopes of finding you," she answered, with that lilt in her voice. He was sitting upright on the bottom bench, and he felt her hand on the top of his head. Was it on purpose? He didn't wait to find out, but reached up and took the hand in the darkness, then turned sideways to sit quietly, with their clasped hands resting on the middle bench between them. In this dark chamber, how remarkably exciting was the touch of her hand! Her thumb moved slowly over his knuckles, and his fingertips felt the contours of her nails. "Talk about perceptual consciousness!" he said.

"Are you getting too hot?" she said, so sweetly he knew she meant it literally.

"In more ways than one," he answered.

"You should cool off in the creek," she offered kindly, "then you could come back in for a little longer. I notice you haven't been doing that."

He hadn't thought of it. But it was a good idea. "Promise not to disappear?" he asked, disengaging his hand.

"Can someone invisible disappear?" she said.

"I don't know, but don't try it."

When he came back in, temporarily refreshed, they held hands again, and he asked her who she was.

"Oh, nobody you've ever heard of."

"You know what I mean. Which person here is you? What's your name? What do you look like?"

"I look like a hand in the dark," she said.

"You're a terrible tease. Let's get out of this sweathole. Let's get born. Let's take a walk together tomorrow."

"I like it better this way," she murmured. "Don't you think it's kind of fun?"

"I can't tell if it's fun or not. I think it's making me a little crazy. At least just give me a hint — What color is your hair? Are you a blonde? A redhead?"

"I'm a figment of your imagination."

"I never knew I had such a powerful imagination."

"It reminds me of Cupid and Psyche," she said.

"I don't remember the story. Will you tell it to me?"

"Well, Cupid took Psyche to live with him in his palace, but she wasn't allowed to see him. And every night he came to bed with her after dark, and left before it was light. She had everything else she wanted, but she had to promise not to try and find out who he was."

"Ah, it's all coming back to me now," he said. "And now I know just how poor Psyche must have felt. But why didn't he want her to see him, anyway?"

"I guess maybe he wanted to be sure she didn't love him just for his beautiful bod. But her mean sisters said he was probably hideous, and that was why she couldn't see him. So one night she couldn't stand it any longer, and after he was asleep she lit the lamp, and she was so surprised to see him, to see the god of love, that she spilled some hot oil on his shoulder and woke him up.

And when he realized she'd broken her promise, he left her."

"Oh, it's so sad. But didn't she get him back in the end?"

"I don't remember."

"How unromantic of you. I'm a terrible sucker for a happy ending. I think she redeemed herself somehow, and they lived happily ever after, dancing hand in hand"—he squeezed her hand—"through the Elysian Fields. But it's the other way around with us—you're the one insisting on a mantle of darkness. And it's harder for me than it was for Psyche."

"Why do you say that?"

"Well for one thing, it's so hot in here. And for another, I think it's more important to a man what a woman looks like than vice versa."

"Oh you do, do you?" She gently pinched each web of skin at the base of his fingers.

"If you tell me your height and weight I'll tell you mine." But the most he could get out of her before he left was her promise to be there the following night. It was both infuriating and exciting.

On Wednesday he was in a state of considerable agitation. The workshop ended on Saturday noon, so it was already half over, and here he was, practically in love with a voice and a hand.

At lunch he sat opposite a black woman with close-cropped hair, broad shoulders, and a serene expression. They ate, as usual, outdoors, on a flagstone terrace, partially shaded by a grape arbor. Even while they ate, jays came to peck at the ripening grapes, and one of the waiters would flap a napkin at them. Instead of the buzz of conversation, their music was the gurgling of the creek, and the clink of cutlery.

He watched the brown hand across from him as it manipulated the fork to spindle a leaf of lettuce and walnut half, pushing far enough into the walnut to make it stick on, but not so far that it would break apart. He marveled at details which he wouldn't have even seen a few days before. The hand raised its perfectly balanced bite to the lips that neatly pulled it off, leaving the fork tines bare and shining in the sun, and then the hand returned the fork in a gentle arc to the salad plate. Remarkable hand! Had he held it? After lunch he retired to his cabin to sleep away the midday heat.

Wednesday was his fourth night in the sauna, and then there would be two more. "Are you here, Ms. Hand?" he asked on entering.

"I'm here. Would you like a back rub tonight?" This was certainly an acceleration! "I know it sounds abrupt, but after all, our time is limited in here."

He lay on his stomach on the bottom bench, and she straddled his legs. From the feel of her weight he guessed that her feet reached the floor on either side, and partly supported her. "Don't burn your feet on the steam," he said. Her hands felt strong, and found their way to muscles that were knotted. Each time she leaned forward to reach his shoulders, he thought he could feel her pubic hair grazing softly against his buttocks. His consciousness kept shifting from the skin beneath her hands to the saddle of skin she sat on.

"This is your line of work, not mine," she said. "I really don't know what I'm doing."

He sang a snatch of an old song: "Just keep on doin' what you're doin', although it's leadin' me to ruin, just keep on doin' what you're doin', 'cause I love what you're doin' to me." His low voice filled up their small envelope of darkness.

"When your pores open up in here, your skin gets really sensitive," she said.

He had to go outside to cool off in the stream. He found a shallow spot, where the cold stream water was warmed by an influence from the hot springs, and he sat still on the rocks of the stream bed and looked up at the sky. There was no moon, but the starlight was so bright here that he could see the dark forms of the mountains, wrapping their arms around him. So she was an astrologer. Between the mountains he saw the Big Dipper, the only constellation he could recognize. Just upstream, by the other saunas, people were laughing and splashing. He went back inside.

"Your friends the stars are out in force tonight," he said.

"Yes? I'm not surprised. They're there in force every night, and all day long, too. You ought to know that just because you can't see them it doesn't mean they're not there."

"How right you are," he said. He offered her a back rub, and she said that she'd been hiking, and what she'd really like was a leg rub. They changed places, only he sat on the bench, just beyond her feet. This was his chance to find out more about her physical form. He put a hand on each Achilles tendon, and slowly started up. Her calves were firm and hairy, unshaven, so she *was* a feminist. The muscles of her calves felt round and strong. The backs and sides of her knees felt smooth, without puckers or protruding veins. Her thighs went on and on. He seemed to move his hands a long time up these columns that were firm and strong, nice and long, before he came to the obstruction of her buttocks. He hesitated a moment, then started back down the way he'd come. Well, she wasn't fat, but she wasn't skinny either. He had time to rub her feet a little, to feel their callouses and long toes, before he pooped out from the heat.

"Will you reveal yourself to me before this thing is over?" he pleaded. Tonight he felt softened, malleable to her whim.

"We'll see," she said.

When he left he was wobbly with suspended excitation.

On Thursday, in his sensitivity session, he worked with a man. There would have been no avoiding it, except by blatant heterosexual chauvinism. As people paired off with whomever stood nearby, he found himself alone in a corner of the room with a slender man, much younger than himself, with a startlingly sensual face and intense hazel eyes. It would be a relief, anyway, not to be wondering the whole time if his partner was the sauna woman.

Today they used little sandbags about six inches square. He gently lowered and raised the bag on different parts of his partner's supine body. He was a little jealous of this man's physical beauty, the tanned forearm he lowered the bag onto, the prominent hip bone under the soft muslin pants, asking to be touched.

When it was his turn, he closed his eyes and waited for the bag's weight, never knowing where it would come next. It was lowered so slowly he couldn't mark the moment when the sensation began. It was a cool weight, that slowly spread itself, like a bare foot on the floor, like water. It came on his shoulder and was gone again; then his forehead felt the silent crescendo, then upper arm, then thigh. The sandbag left no gaps, but filled like a liquid the surface it covered. He was breathing hard, his whole body tuned expectantly to the next touch. The pause seemed infinite — his partner was apparently varying the rhythm — but there it was, spreading out over his abdomen. With a lurch his sentience shifted, the unnameable excitement sought a nameable form: he was getting an erection. Damn it, anyway, he couldn't just lie there with a beautiful young man kneeling beside him while his cock stood up in his loose-fitting pants and waved to the roomful of people. The unexpected loss of control was as unnerving to him as the embarrassment. So before the situation got out of hand, he stood up abruptly, smiled an apology to his partner, rubbed his stomach as if to say he felt ill, and fled from the room. He felt like an adolescent.

In the afternoon, he went for a short hike with his colleague. He needed to talk to somebody from the real world, get a grip on himself. "How do you like the workshop?" he asked his friend.

"It's an excuse to be here. I think most of this business with bean bags and so on is a waste of time, though. It's a little too cute for me. I don't get off on it — Do you?"

"Yes, in a way. I'm surprised how much of an effect the exercises and everything have on me. And besides, a funny thing's been happening." He picked a sprig of sage from the side of the path, crushed it between his fingers and held it to his nose. "I've been meeting a woman in the sauna every night, but I've never seen her. It's so bizarre. Last night she gave me a back rub."

"Isn't it a little hot in there for that kind of hanky-panky?" said his friend.

"Yes — I nearly fainted last night. Watch the poison oak there."

"Well, I've found a hidden boulder that serves the purpose very well. Have you noticed the little redhead?" This with a significant wink.

"More power to you," he said, feeling irritated. "I hope you don't both get covered with poison oak, or bitten by rattlesnakes."

His friend laughed goodnaturedly. "It would almost be worth it."

"At first I though the woman in the sauna might be the redhead," he continued, "but now I know she's not — don't worry. The woman in the sauna is bigger. But she won't tell me who she is."

"No doubt she has her reasons," said his friend sarcastically. "Some physical imperfection, perhaps. An extra nose or mouth. The sauna's a great place for a girl like that."

"Don't be so flippant," he said hotly. "I don't care

how many noses she's got. There's something very
beautiful about her. I don't know how I know it, but I
know it."

"Hey, man, take it easy! I was only kidding. You
know what an unregenerate male chauvinist I am. Take
me with a grain of salt."

They dropped the subject, and for the rest of their
walk the conversation turned on clinic gossip, and the
fact that their program director was moving to L.A. to
open a new clinic, and hoped to take two staff members
with him.

"I'm thinking of going," he said. "I love San Francisco, but you know my kids are in L.A. now, and I'd
like to be close to them."

In the middle of the path there was a big snake with
black and white stripes, coiled in the sun. "It's a king
snake," he told his friend. "They're harmless—to people." It waited, motionless, till they got very close,
before slithering away into the sagebrush.

When he entered the sauna on Thursday, his first
impression was that the room was much cooler than
usual. The voice was already there. Did she think it was
cooler? Yes, when she'd arrived just a few minutes
before, the heavy door had been propped open with a
stone.

"This coolness gives us more time together," he said.
"Let me massage you first, tonight." She lay on the middle bench, on her back, and he variously kneeled and
squatted on the bench below. "I'm putting you together
in bits and pieces, like a jigsaw puzzle," he said, as his
kneading hands felt their way up the side of her torso, a
roller coaster ride of swelling hip and slender waist.

By the time he got to her breasts, his perceptions had
grown blurry. He couldn't tell, for example, whether her
breasts felt large or small; he only knew they felt good.
Still, he was careful at this stage to go around the nipples.

"Is this what you call body work?" she asked.

A little later, his hands had transgressed all boundaries, and she was eager as he. How smoothly they had moved ahead.

"But what if someone comes in?" she asked, in an attack of modesty.

"Then we'll just be quiet, and keep on doin' what we're doin', whatever that is. Besides, nobody will come in."

He straddled the middle bench, and she sat facing him, on his lap. The trouble was, there was nothing to push against or hold on to up here in the bleachers except each other. Their legs dangled like children's legs from grown-up chairs. He was suddenly ashamed of his thoughtlessness. "I should have asked before," he said, "but what do you do for birth control?"

"I use lunarception," she answered. It crossed his mind then that she might be downright nuts, like some ancient Delphic priestess who'd watched at her crack of steam till she'd gone mad with the vapors. Well, whatever lunarception was, he wasn't going to ask her about it now. They rocked quietly back and forth, unanchored in the dark, till he felt a swelling vertigo that made everything else shrink. He was afraid he'd faint and fall down between the benches.

"I'm sorry," he said, "but I'm awfully dizzy all of a sudden. I think I'd better stop."

"Me too," she said sweetly. "I've been trying not to faint." So she was no sorceress after all, but an ordinary being like himself.

They slipped apart and he took her face in his hands, and finally kissed her. She had only one mouth, one nose. The hair around her face was fuzzed out from the heat, and at the back of her head it was twisted into a knot.

"I guess it's not so easy to make love in the sauna," she said.

"We might have much better luck out of the sauna.

Won't you let me see you, you sweet one?"

"Are you sure you really want to?"

"Is there some reason I wouldn't?"

"Only that it would destroy what we have. I've never done this before either, you know."

"But aren't you even a little curious about me?"

"Of course I'm curious. That's what makes it exciting. But maybe on Saturday, when the workshop's over—"

At breakfast on Friday he sat beside a woman in her fifties. Ordinarily he wouldn't have noticed anything except her age, but this morning he looked intently at her and found her lovely. Her gray hair was rolled neatly into a French twist. She turned to ask him, by silent gesture, for the hot cinnamon-nut rolls and caught him staring at her. She met his eyes with an unflinching gaze that was, perhaps, a sign. Yes, it could be her; anything was possible, certainly that. He purposely dropped his napkin and leaned down to pick it up, but she was wearing slacks, so he couldn't tell if her legs were hairy or not.

During the morning session he sat on the floor opposite a tall woman with long brown hair. Her body looked like a dancer's; its fine muscle tone glowed through her leotard and tights. But her face was badly scarred and reddened by acne. With their legs outstretched, they rolled a ball back and forth between them, from crotch to crotch, like tiny children. As he leaned forward to release the ball, she leaned back, receiving, and so they rocked back and forth in rhythm. He felt his spine curve to suit the action, echoing the roundness of the ball. A feeling of déja-vu came over him, and then he identified its source: last night's rocking in the sauna. He studied his partner's face, and she flashed him a smile.

She responded to his movements in perfect rhythm, so that they moved as one. He loved her for her responsiveness, and for being someone he could be responsive to; he didn't care if she had a bad complexion.

When he got to the sauna on Friday night, the door was held open by a stone, and there was nobody inside. He closed the door behind him, and sat on the bottom bench, crosslegged—to keep his feet up off the hot floor. He was afraid she wouldn't come, and he began to prepare himself for the disappointment. What nonsense it all was, anyway. He'd been behaving like a kid. His pores ought to be clean enough by now.

But she came in, and it didn't seem like nonsense after all. "Hi, beautiful," he said. "I sure am glad to see you. You're looking especially lovely tonight." They sat together on the middle bench. "Just tell me one thing," he said after a minute. "Are you the woman I worked with in this morning's session, with the ball?"

"Oh no," she said. "Didn't I tell you? They switched me to the afternoon group. To even the numbers."

Again he held her on his lap, but this time he sat facing the door, on the top bench, with his back against the wall and his feet on the bench below. It was a much more stable position. "I don't care anymore what you look like," he whispered in her ear. "I *know* you're beautiful."

"At an inopportune moment the door creaked open. "Anyone in this inferno?" said the voice of his colleague. He couldn't answer, or he'd have to make conversation. "You answer him," he hissed in her ear.

"Yes," she said over her shoulder, just a little breathily. "There's two of us up here on the top bench."

"Okeydoke," said his friend. "I'll just sit down here in the dugout."

In spite of his bold promises, he found it hard to keep on doin' what they had been doin'. He felt constrained, afraid his knees would pop, or he'd make an involuntary grunt. The darkness no longer felt like a cloak to him. They both sat motionless, except for the silent squeezing of her vaginal muscles.

"Well, shoot," said the colleague, "it's not hot enough in here for me. I'll try one of the other saunas."

When he closed the door behind him, it came as a great relief to both of them. And before they parted, she promised to meet him at the resort office, at noon the following day, after the close of the workshop.

The next morning he saw his colleague on the path, who asked with a wink, "How's life going in the sauna?"

"Oh, fine, thanks."

"I took a sauna last night," said the friend, "but the first one I went into spooked me. There were two people in there, apparently, but all they did was breathe. I got the feeling they were actually balling. Of course I don't think it's *wrong,* just bad style. Sweating like pigs, they must have been. It wasn't you, was it?"

"Oh, no."

By 11:30 his car was packed and he was ready to go. He was nervous about the forthcoming meeting. He wanted to like her, wanted her to like him. Maybe they'd spend the afternoon together, go to the beach at Big Sur, before going their separate ways. True, she lived in L.A. But he really might move there; anything could happen. He went to the office and paid his bill, then sat down in the corner and pretended to read, but every time someone came into the office to check out, his heart wriggled around inside. The gray-haired woman came in. "How much do I owe you?" she said to the clerk, in a gentle but unfamiliar voice. After that he forced himself not to look up with each set of footsteps, but just to wait until he heard the voice—his voice. There was a strange man's voice, then his colleague's voice. He had to look up and nod a greeting, hoping the colleague would leave quickly, for somehow he didn't want him to witness the meeting between him and his new friend. But the colleague hurried away again, in his habitual hustle and bustle. Then there was a strange woman's voice, and then there was the voice of the sauna, saying, "Hi—I'm Diana Waters, cabin 8. What do I owe you?"

He looked up from the shadowed alcove by the door, and saw her from the side. She didn't see him. She was a long-legged woman with long black hair, let loose down her back. Her white shirt of embroidered Indian cotton contrasted with her tanned olive skin and black hair. The shirt was tucked into snugly fitting jeans that showed a small waist and a smooth behind. She had high cheekbones, large eyes, long lashes, a small mouth, a slightly pointed chin. He saw all this in a flash—saw in the blink of an eye that she was perfect; unbearably so. How he loved her, and, thanks to her, all womankind! How good she'd been to him, with his bad teeth and his one-track mind. Feeling dizzy, he grabbed his book and slipped silently from the office to his car.

Engagement

Steve Wiesinger

she rolls onto her shoulders
                    yoga-style
            she is naked
                the soft line
                    of her sex
                            parted
            because it is her pleasure
                    and mine
the dish of her hips
                opens to the night
            and in the within
                I can sense lake
                        and basin
            emptiness
                    and bay
        sense the way fate might
                    push through
                    the pink center
these inlets and coves
            resiliant shoreline
                    of our love

Field

Olga Broumas

I had a lover. Let us say we were married, owned a house, shared a car. The trees were larch, white birch, maple, poplar and pine, the mountains granite, and two months of the year verdantly lush. We met cows, sheep and horses on our walks up or downhill a fine dirt road. In time, my lover came to take another lover, of whom I also became enamored. There is a seagull floating backward in a rare snowstorm on an Atlantic ocean bay as I remember this, its head at an angle that suggests amusement. This younger lover flew home to a far Southern state and returned in a large car with several rare instruments and a great Dane, a very spirited animal, who had to be returned to a family estate in the midwest soon thereafter, having discovered and devoured a neighboring farmer's chickens. The seagull flies laboriously into the wind the length of my windows then settles to be floated back. It is a young bird, wings black-tipped and grey. We added a room to the cabin that summer, the work done by a young sculptor from the college, one who seemed to be continuously counting, a devotional attitude that appealed to me. One evening we returned to find a note pinned to our door Call Ted abt. a possible free piano. That it did not materialize did not affect my feelings toward him and in September I moved my area into this room. It was, in many ways, the perfect abode. Fifteen by seventeen, it had a long

wall of old windows, grey from years without paint, a
door with a sturdy ladder to the forest floor, a small
stove, a wall of the enormous cedar logs of the main
cabin and, to it, a soundproof door with a double window Ted had devised. Our younger lover took over my
old area, and my lover continued working upstairs in
the bedroom where the rising heat from the Franklin
caused her to take off her clothes frequently as well as
open a window. We bought a large futon for my room,
and next to it laid a smaller futon, what is called a yoga
mat, turned the quilts sideways and slept facing the
luminous birches in differing night lights. Enormous
fireflies when the temperature hovers at thirty near midnight, early September, late June. Daylight was often a
wrathful time, and it is a tribute to the height of our
spirits that we barely noticed, gliding over it as we did
over friends and professions. The phenomenon of three
hearts dilating as if forever in unison, the eyes diverging
to offer this to each one, rare, blasted our systems with
tremendous energy, and within the year we packed each
a bag, compromised on five instruments, of which two
collapsible, and a small amp, and flew to a continent
where one of us knew one country's language. We
traveled, fought, separated and reunited for six months,
at which time we were joined by an old friend traveling
with whom we thought a lover, but who turned out to be
a companion, a tall, stately model with the gait, approaching us on the beach, of a sulky seven-year-old.
Our younger lover's age, they played music together,
and together got stranded midsea in an inflatable boat
whose outboard motor they'd flooded. I sacrifice myself
to the sea, chants our lover, unforgettable in this scene
if unwitnessed, as the model fumbles with the four flim-
sy oars and Row, damn it! They made it to shore half a
mile east of our house, and were towed by a small speedboat belonging to a man who had tried to fix their
motor, he standing in the fiberglass, they sitting behind,

past the entire village on their wooden chairs outside the grocery, the eating house, the front garden doors. The model was extremely cheerful at dinner, having hauled the canvas tub to the yard, our lover wounded in pride and spiteful. We lived in that house on the edge of the water for two months, until our money ran out and we returned to our wooded hill, my friend and companion to their town by the Eastern tip of a Finger Lake, seven hours by car further inland. My lover and I found that our jobs during our leave had been embittered by our firm's acquisition by a larger establishment affiliated with the military. We resigned, or rather, refused the new firm's offer, and shortly thereafter moved to my friend's town where I accepted a federally funded position that made use of my skills in music and massage, a divergence that delighted me. We rented a farm out of town, partly on work-exchange, feeding and caring for two horses, two dogs, one of them slightly mad, six cats and a senile bunny. This our lover agreed to do, as well as stacking most of the nine cords in a fit of jealousy every morning the week my lover was in California. They were actually face-cords, the pile would have measured four and a half in our old county. They made a terrific racket, hurled across the yard into the barn where the dogs from their pen greeted them. The farm was off a straight North-South road, they couldn't be trusted loose in the four-wheel-drive traffic, they were rough barn animals and couldn't be kept in the house, but their barking from their large, humane, indoor-out pen with running brook and bales of hay had an ungraceful sound that made us ignore the fence when they broke it, to the chagrin and later vituperation of the owner who kept our deposit. My lover returned from California with three bottles of fine red, one of them a Petite Sirah, striped underwear and purple velour tops for us, and the seedling of a new self profoundly and coincidentally engendered during a brief affair with the

lover I'd left to move East to our cabin. Our younger
lover didn't recognize the smell under the fingernails as I
did, with pleasure. It is impossible to disengage from
jealousy, someone told me in graduate school. It
challenged me to find an act that wouldn't feed it and
have put my mind to it since, profiting only from a
general graciousness, nonchalance, fatality. The
snowfall that winter was heavy and the winds tore
savagely to one side of our four mile road. By what
should have been mid-spring our lover had contrived to
be collected to the faraway Southern state, and we did
not care to pursue the deposit. Though we were broke, a
sensation like shutters beating bodily in the stillness that
followed the April winds preoccupied us exclusively,
though I did see the lilacs crashing it seemed through the
old barn walls, and the hill go green on the stain of the
belly-shot doe before it snowed. We moved, with my
friend, to California for a summer job arranged by my
old lover, and the four of us passed those months
specifically amiably, in fairly rigid pair formation, I and
my friend, who had first become my lover under my
younger lover's hand while abroad by the sea, a gesture
delicate and precise, savored by all and regretted bitterly
and immediately by the youngest, my old lover and my
lover. We lived and worked, teaching nutrition, healing
and survival skills to young adults, in what had been a
Navy compound on a Pacific coast beach, and had long
hours of simple sitting, and staring. I brought my guitar
and practiced hearing in detail my picking against the
foghorns and gulls. My lover sang. My friend was a little insecure far from home and clung, peacefully, to my
middle. In the fall we moved to be half the staff at the
halfway house here. The pay was low but secure, and we
each rented a studio facing the bay for the off season.
We did not travel together. Rather, my lover flew directly, my old lover via the midwest to visit family, and my
friend and I drove the car. Snow Creek, Lake Crescent,

Ruby Beach, Humptulips, Tokeland, Palix, Parpala,
Hug Point, Arch Cape, Perpetua, Darlingtonia, Bliss
14, Pacific Fruit Express, Grace, Power County, Sweet-
water, Harmony, Adora, Amana, Homewood,
Vermillion, Presque Isle. We've lived here four months,
a full holiday season, friends from inland and the West.
My lover and I bicycle the dune roads to the ocean. The
winter is mild, and the bay home to seven varieties of
duck that I've sighted, and seagulls and pipers and
pigeons that stop on the railing to hear the guitar and
are annoyed and scold and shift if I should lose my con-
centration for their flattery. My friend and I cook meals
for our festivities, and make love for exquisite hours
when I may scream and contort myself but on leaving
the house remember nothing, no, not nothing exactly. I
remember if put to it, but not ordinarily. My old lover
and I are affectionate, my lover and I are cheery, and
our younger lover recovered and moved to a large city
nearby among old college friends and infrequently visits
my lover, and lately, lightly, me.

Blue Creamer

J. Kelly

If you were an antique blue creamer in the shape of a cow I'd fill you with fresh cream every morning and drink it from you all day long.

If ya was a navy bean I'd scoop ya outa my bowl an put ya in my pocket so's I could stick my hand in there an pet ya with my thumb.

If you were a white and purple rug with green swirls I'd put you in the sun and pour sweet oil on my body and open my arms and legs and lie on you.

If ya was ta cry I'd hold ya in my lap an touch the back a yer neck an tell ya stories. If ya was ta laugh I'd kiss yer eyes an nose an chin an the top a yer head.

If you were my lover I'd take you to the garden and plant you deep in the sweet black soil. I would take you down so slowly there are miles of sky between you and the earth a bed of bone and flesh hair blood teeth lips tongue I plant myself in you.

Red Zinger

Michael Frome

Jane asked about the explosion of sounds they heard at twilight in the wild, but Mark didn't know much more about it than she did. It takes a lot of time and a lot of listening to fathom music, whether performed by professional musicians on human-made instruments or by water, wind or wild animals. But if Jane wanted an answer, she should have one.

"I think we hear the critters up here crooning in love, or calling for mates, or maybe challenging one another to conflict. Or singing and shouting about another day of life on earth." Mark wasn't sure that made sense, though he felt there must be some inherent rhythm, beyond human understanding, and that he and Jane were part of it.

They were riding their horses to observe sunset from a high ridge above camp on Pelican Creek. They had been through a long day on the trail, but still craved more, and found it in the moments they now spent together as western skies darkened. Mark followed the soft white and gradient blues and bronzes, light and shadow of fading day merging with oncoming night under a waxing moon, nearly full.

In virtually every meadow a herd of elk fed undisturbed. They rode past a massive old bison feeding alone on clover and grasses. I sense kinship with that bull, Mark murmured to his inner self, for we both are solitary characters in the eventide of our lives; this little romance on the trail is a brief interlude at best, for her as well as me, and let's not think of it as anything more.

Jane at that moment pointed to three coyotes scouting the edges of an elk herd, evidently ready to pick off one that might be weak or stray. As they rode they listened intently to twilight songs, mostly but not altogether of elk, variously shrill, soft, groaning, cooing, and melodic and harmonic in their own way. It was a little too shadowy to see Jane's features clearly, beyond her finely chiseled nose and chin, and they in silhouette mostly. The world for the moment stood still; it was complete, without a yesterday or tomorrow. He pictured them fleetingly in bed—in a sleeping bag, really—their two bodies as one. Physical "beauty," as normally measured in the world out there, had absolutely no meaning.

Jane reached out to touch his hand while they looked across Yellowstone's forests, the thermal vapors rising like clouds and Yellowstone Lake reflecting the alpenglow. Then they turned back to camp, tended to the horses and finally crawled in their domed tent, colored blue and gold, for a night of full romance. Jane was scarcely out of his arms, her lithe, light body fitting snugly and weightlessly against his. Though the ground was hard, it couldn't have mattered less.

Now and then during the night Mark would listen to the breeze, or become conscious of the horses, hobbled at the ankles to keep them close, feeding on grass where they could find it, or picture buffalo and grizzly exploring the neighborhood. But then Jane would touch him and all sounds were forgotten. She wanted to be held. The passion of intercourse was fulfilling, but what Jane wanted was to be wanted, enveloped in his willing arms.

Mark hadn't experienced such passion in a long time, certainly not since his wife, Verna, had died. There had been other women, not many but a few in the five years that he'd been alone, though none to stir the fire. Was it the woman? Or the setting? Or something inside himself come to life anew? He remembered his honeymoon of long ago, when he and Verna had gone to the Caribbean, scuba diving and romancing underwater at Jamaica, then camping at Guadeloupe in the French West Indies. What a mistake that had been — trying to camp in a rain forest! — yet he recalled with pleasure Verna bathing in the buff under a waterfall, washing her long blonde hair and looking as natural as the day she was born.

How do I, he wondered, look to women without anything but my birthday suit? He was nearing sixty, of medium height and build, with blue eyes behind his bifocals; broad, ruddy face, not especially handsome, and wavy brown hair, already receded yet gray only around the temples. Mark was a professor of journalism, who actually had been a columnist and editor on newspapers years before, now teaching, or trying to teach, students who had difficulty in spelling, punctuation and grammar, and scant aspiration to follow the footsteps of Lincoln Steffens. He devoured a variety of periodicals and did some writing on journalism ethics and objectivity, or what he considered the fallacy in the assumption of objectivity. Generally he preferred the companionship of men rather than women, especially when traveling in the out-of-doors.

But Mark liked to sample a variety of experiences. Thus for this particular summer he had joined a one-week horse pack trip into the Yellowstone country. It was an expensive type of vacation, but Mark enjoyed riding without the responsibilities of camp cooking and caring for horses. He'd been to Yellowstone before, at least three or four times, but never to the Mirror Plateau, a wilderness portion of the park frontiers removed from the standard loop that millions of tourists cover yearly.

The trail riders met each other at Silver Gate, near

the east entrance of the park and their horses soon after at Soda Butte in the Lamar Valley. In contrast with Mammoth Hot Springs, West Yellowstone, Yellowstone Lake or Old Faithful—the majority of activity centers—traffic was light, virtually nonexistent. There wasn't much difference between the terrain in the Lamar Valley and bordering Montana, except the national park label. People behave differently, thought Mark, but animals, vegetables and minerals don't care about boundaries.

They were a group of nine riders, he noted, as they started on the trail which climbed from grassland and sagebrush through fields of wildflowers and pine forests. They paused along the way to scan rocky ranges reaching to the horizons in Wyoming and Montana. This was Yellowstone, as it was meant to be, a sanctuary in which these visitors could easily consider themselves to be the intruders.

Jane sat at the end of the log in front of the fire, putting down her dinner plate when she and Mark had their first conversation. The outfitter, Walt, and his wife, Nancy, sidekick and cook, wanted to get people talking. Walt himself, bred on a Wyoming ranch, had little to say; he was hobbled from too many spills as a youthful rodeo rider, but clearly knew the country and his horses. Twenty years ago Nancy had come west as a dude from Rhode Island and never went back. She was engaged in dialogue with an older couple from her home state, small talk about names and places with little meaning to anyone else. "I'm from northern California," said Mark to Jane. "How about you?"

She appeared to be about forty, not unattractive, but cool, reserved, either quite self-assured or perhaps insecure and defensive, playing the role of the loner—somewhat like Mark himself. The lady is young still, but not so young, he thought. Her fingers were slender but far from delicate; she had working hands, toughened in a profession or in homekeeping, or in both. Her eyes were greenish-blue, defiant and independent. Her skin was smooth but pale and her short blondish-brown hair was graying. She did nothing to project a come-hither image, yet there was something appealing or challenging in her. She was from Evanston, outside of Chicago, was in education too, a nurse teaching advanced nursing and studying for her doctorate. Long after, Mark would remember that she had brought her own herbal tea and had shared, rather reluctantly, her Red Zinger.

The scene livened abruptly when the grizzly bear made its appearance. Walt spotted it first about one hundred yards outside of camp. It was curious but kept its distance, doubtless sniffing the aroma of the meal the group had just finished. It was larger than a cub but not yet full-grown.

"Who wants to saddle up and ride for a closer look?" asked Walt. The older couple from Rhode Island declined; they were working on their post-dinner Scotches (which followed their pre-dinner Scotches). So did Laurel, the buxom sexy Texas lady in her fifties, and the dark-haired twins, young women from upstate New York, who had little experience in riding. That left Jane, who was up for the ride, and Mark. But the pursuit was complicated by the fact that the horses were unsaddled and out to pasture. "We'll take two horses," decided Mark. "I'll ride Midnight and you two get on Buster. He's a big old boy that bear won't spook."

They never got close to the bear, but Jane got close to Mark, her arms holding tightly around his waist while they galloped over the meadow. She wasn't very large or heavy, no more than five feet four and possibly 105 to 110 pounds. He could tell she was sliding around Buster's back end and doing her best to stay on board. Mark wasn't overly confident himself, but the feel of her body was stimulating. He felt her hanging on for dear life. Her breasts pressed against him and her arms clasped around his waist. She was no longer the epitome of independence. This was Mark's moment, if he was up to it and able to contain his own fear.

The bear took to the brush and they returned to camp. Twilight shadows crossed the meadows, while daylight lingered. Mark and Jane walked among the four or five tents scattered in the grove of trees and beyond it to a rocky outcrop. Views unfolded of the great ranges surrounding Yellowstone: the Beartooth and Snowy ranges, the Gallatin Mountains, the Absarokas, and the snowy Tetons far to the south, dramatic because they rise stark and sharp from the valley floor.

"I wonder why we've all come on a trip like this. Is it to sit out here and see this particular sight?" asked Mark. "Is it something of the past we're looking for—a frontier as it must have been a century ago, of space and solitude? There must be some easier way of deriving pleasure. Or is there?"

"I don't think it's important to have the answers," responded Jane. "I budgeted and saved to come here. It's wonderful to be free of motorized sounds and beyond reach of civilization, or what we call civilization."

She went on to explain that she gave herself the trip as a present to celebrate her divorce after nineteen years of marriage and two children. Her ex-husband was a successful broker in Chicago, successful in everything but his relations with his wife and family. They had married very early, before she was twenty. "I could almost say that I went directly from puberty to motherhood, without having the fun of growing up. Now I know that I can be my own person. I feel so free, or, as the song goes, 'free at last, free at last!'"

Silently, they watched a golden eagle riding thermal currents above them. Jane lay back on the rock studying the eagle and the blue sky above it. Mark felt moved by her openness and was glad that he hadn't judged her harshly when they first met. It struck him that people erect false barriers and that in the wild country life becomes simpler and free of artifice. If there were only the two of them, suddenly lost and cut off from the rest of the party, how would they make out? Would they pull together or apart? What sort of partner would she prove if the going got rough? For that matter, what sort would he be? Can loners learn to care and share or must they forever be focused on their own needs and wants?

Mark began to fill the silence.

"Birds do a lot of things in the air that we humans can do only on the ground. They have mating rituals in flight, romancing that we don't really understand, and copulation too. Prairie chickens, I'm told, go through a great mating dance out on the prairie, which I'd love to see sometime.

"Once I sailed with a friend through the Channel Islands, off the coast of Santa Barbara. On the most distant island, San Miguel, we watched huge elephant seals come in out of the sea. Imagine, if you can, one elephant seal mounting another. It doesn't happen fast — and it's not easy.

"Another time I was on the East Coast, at Bull Island, off South Carolina, where I watched sea turtles come in to lay their eggs. A chore if ever there was one. I mean, these are sea creatures, waddling on land very slowly as I suppose their ancestors must have done when they came out for the first time millions of years ago. Then each digs a hole, lays its eggs, covers the hole and waddles back to the sea. The eggs are white, and shaped like ping pong balls. I was up all night watching the turtles come and go. I kept counting eggs per turtle. Some dropped more than 150. They cry during the process, with tears streaming down their watery faces. The experts say it's because of the strain involved. Maybe so, or could there be something more involved?"

Mark looked at Jane, but her eyes were closed; she was either daydreaming or sleeping and hadn't heard a word he said. Had he talked too much and tried to be too smart? Mark lay back on the rock with his shoulder touching hers, sensing that she was conscious of it but not repelled. Without aggressiveness, he let a hand lay against her side. She put her hand in his. He squeezed it lightly and she responded. Mark rolled on his side, embracing her with both arms and drawing her close. They clung to each other and kissed, then rose to walk quietly back to Mark's tent, pitched on the outer edge of the trees. He was sleeping alone, while everyone else in the group was paired, Jane with Laurel, the Texas lady.

Jane spent the entire night with Mark. It was her coming-out party, as she later explained. Her husband had been the first man she'd been to bed with (before they were married) and the only one she'd been to bed with before Mark. They nestled in his sleeping bag, their arms and torsos and cheeks and lips hardly ever out of contact.

After that first night she had announced, "I'm moving in with you. I've talked with Laurel and she thinks it's a great idea. We'll find a spot where we can pitch the tent and be alone." Thus began a lovely wilderness romance, sharing days as well as nights. They observed herds of elk and buffalo in their summer range of high, lush meadows, an occasional moose, grouse and coyote. They saw different kinds of birds, the species varying with elevation and terrain: bald eagle and rare black rose finch, birds of striking form and elegant beauty such as the sandhill crane, trumpeter swan and scarlet tanager. For almost a week their little party didn't see another human while they rode through glacier-carved valleys and alpine meadows abloom with Indian paintbrush and lupine.

Jane smiled more. She joked with Mark. "You're going to meet a wild western woman tonight — and that's me!" she exclaimed one morning while they were brushing their teeth together near (but not too near) a lovely little stream. She wore a faded pair of jeans and broad-brimmed western hat and looked bred for the role. Mark wondered, but not for long, what she'd be like in city dress: everything here was complete in itself.

Mark was proud to find Jane a good rider and camper. They shared days with the others, though they could tell that each day brought the two of them closer together. They were companions on the trail, climbing spiny mountain ridges, then zigzagging down switchbacks into meadows and river valleys. Only a few were officially designated trails; Walt had chosen well-trodden wildlife routes, or made his own. During the day Jane was one person, deriving the most from Yellowstone, hiking, riding, pitching in with chores, enthusiastic yet still a little reserved. Throughout the night she was another person, making the most of being with Mark, scarcely out of his arms. Mark found out something about himself: that he was able to give love and receive it. Their blue and gold tent became their own little blue and gold spaceship as they traveled into orbit.

They could have remained in Yellowstone forever. At one campsite they stayed two nights, settling for day rides and avoiding the complications of breaking and setting up camp. Mornings were cold and crisp, but when they opened the tent flap they saw buffalo in the meadows, a dozen or more, huge animals grazing gently, undisturbed and undisturbing. Mark would tell Jane now and then that she ought to see the high spots as well—Old Faithful, the mud pots, Yellowstone Lake, Grand Canyon of the Yellowstone River—along with the crowds that come from all over the world. But no, thank you, this would be Yellowstone for her, the way she had always pictured it. It was refreshing for Mark to see this country with her and through her eyes. It was the Yellowstone of limitless distances, of sagebrush desert, open meadow, and high forest; the forest of trees rather than timber, allowed to die and decompose, to the forester's despair; of rocky places, where minerals lie undisturbed, to the geologist's despair; of grasses reserved for wild animals rather than for domestic livestock; of fumaroles, bubbling hot springs, and mud spots of scalding water and superheated steam, yielding the earth's energy free and unfettered; every part of Yellowstone vibrant, alive and changing.

One day they headed for the hot springs, the whole party to bathe in the altogether. The basin was one of those wonders of Yellowstone, reflecting heat and pressure inside the earth. After hiking around bubbling paint pots, pools of boiling water, and spouting geysers that few park visitors get to see, Walt brought the group to the pool of hot water he had promised. It was fed by two streams. One, flowing from some distant, mysterious underground source, furnished hot water, too hot for comfort. Fortunately, it mixed with a clear, cold stream, and the temperature could be adjusted with a barrier log regulating the flow of cold, all providing a soothing interlude, thoroughly welcome after several days of riding and camping.

The Rhode Island couple has no reluctance about bathing in the buff. They may have been older, but were contemporary. Laurel, the sexy Texan, was contemporary too, but definitely more appealing with her clothes on. Walt proved scrawny and raw-boned, an unglamorous figure. Nancy, his partner, had clear eyes and a slender, erect figure, but she was bony and burned from a hard summer on the trail. For the first time Mark saw his tentmate without clothing—until now they'd been naked together only in the dark. She was slender but not small-boned, well proportioned with slender hips. Her breasts were small, on the wrinkled side somehow and not especially appealing, yet he watched her with pleasure, soaping herself easily and gracefully, plainly enjoying the luxury of warm water. The dark-haired twins bathed quietly, though without any show of modesty. Their skins were smooth, breasts small and firm, stomachs flat and free of strains of childbirth. They were unaffected, as children of nature should be, at home in the wild. Mark felt conscious of the sensuous quality of the group bathing, without feeling anything evil about it.

Wild nature, he concluded, is enriched by sensuality, a part of the rhythms and mosaic of life; the ways of the wild must somehow comprise a rational form and continuum, whether or not humankind understands it. If valid for other species, so too should love in the wilderness be for ours, whether in a tent at eight thousand feet, or in a waterfall, or in a coral reef fifty feet below the surface.

Jane considered Mark a bit of a romantic. She was, after all, studying for a doctorate and consequently immersed in statistics and what are called scientific research methods, whereby all conclusions must be demonstrated with acceptably valid data.

"You may be right," Mark conceded, "but once, while preparing an article about trees in the forest, I got to pondering about their sexability and whether they got any thrill out of engaging in the act of procreation. I recall consulting a forest scientist of some standing, who looked at me as though I were stupid for thinking that trees might have feelings of any kind. He was being rational, scientific and objective. Then I read John Muir's account of climbing a tree in Yosemite at the height of a wind storm. He felt that tree had personality and purpose; he wrote that while trees may not make extensive journeys, they do travel. William Bartram, the early botanist, loved plants too, as 'sentient beings.' Maybe the scientists are like tourists intent on driving from Point A to Point B, taking a few snapshots without allowing time to absorb something that could be deeper than facts."

As for Mark and Jane, they had only begun to sense Yellowstone's limitless recesses, but at least they had slowed down to let impressions penetrate. They had only begun to know each other, though the relationship was deeper and stronger than a casual holiday romance. The last night on the trail, while he stroked her graying blondish hair, she cried in his arms, lamenting the prospect of parting.

At the last kiss and embrace when the trip ended, her eyes filled with love and longing. Mark felt they would be going separate ways into separate worlds, that in no way could he be as appealing in Evanston as in Yellowstone. She was bright, youthful, with the best of a professional career ahead of her. He'd come into her life when she yearned for endearment. But to pursue it further — no, in due course she'd identify his abundant weaknesses, leading only to discontent and sadness for them both. It would be better to treasure the interlude as complete in itself.

Jane telephoned his office at the college, but he didn't return the call. When she wrote him his first instinct was not to open the letter, but he did. "I love you more than loving," it began. He decided to read no further. For him it ended when it ended. The hot water was on for tea. He crossed his office, reached for the pot on the counter, poured a cupful and dropped in a bag of Red Zinger.

The Waking

Alice LaBelle

The minute Georgianna spotted the white ferry boat in Piraeus, she knew she was headed for excitement. Four hours later, when she saw the Spetsai harbor from her watch at the railing, a line of open carriages decorating its sun drenched quay, she sensed she'd chosen the perfect island to spend the last three days of her vacation, a sorely needed reprieve from too much ambition.

In Athens her green eyes and copper hair had been a magnet to men. As she'd made her way through the streets to her Syntagma Square hotel, a young man had thrown her a kiss, another held out his arms to her in a mock embrace, still another stepped up with half lowered lids to offer his services.

She'd had her share of male attention, but nothing like this. They seemed obsessed with sex, exuberantly masculine. At night in the Plaka, as she passed between glowing walls under a star-choked sky, their soft voices called to her. "Kanome parea?"

But it wasn't until she saw him from the rail of the ferry boat, as he maneuvered his open carriage into the Spetsai harbor, reins held high, his forearms straining to control the spirited team, that the creature in her was thoroughly shaken and aroused from its deep sea bed.

His skin was bronzed, his hair the color of wheat. He was long in the torso, his muscles firm and full. She

watched him swing down from his seat with controlled
grace, secure the carriage to the hitching post, pat the
flanks of his chestnut team and pause to press each muz-
zle to his cheek. She watched him walk away, his step
feather light for a man his size.

On the dock a crowd of people waited to greet
passengers, among them children calling out rooms for
rent. One of them caught her eye. He was about nine or
ten, small for his age, his body thin but sturdy, his skin
brown as a nut. He was grinning at one of the dock
workers who had reached out for him as he tried to slip
under the mooring ropes. The worker shouted for him
to keep back, holding him by the neck and tousling his
hair.

He was by her side as she stepped from the landing
platform.

"Okay," she said. He took her pack from her hand,
and tugged at her satchel. "No, no," she smiled, slinging
it over her shoulder. They worked their way through the
crowd past the cafes fronting the harbor, turning up onto a main street that led into the neighborhoods above.

Georgianna was glad she was travelling light. She
wanted nothing to hold her down. The climb was long
and steep, past whitewashed garden walls spilling with
bougainvillea and hibiscus.

She entered a courtyard near the top of the hill, a
few paces behind the boy, who had climbed the wide
street like a goat, stopping from time to time to look
back at her. He vanished into the house. "Mama," she
heard him call imperiously.

A big-boned, heavy-set woman with a handsome
face emerged from the door and hurried across the
courtyard, wiping her wet hands on her apron. "Elate,
elate," she called to Georgianna, pulling her sachel from
her hand, motioning for her to follow. Georgianna
noted with satisfaction that the door to the room
opened directly onto the courtyard. As they went

toward it, the woman stopped suddenly and snapped a bloom from a pot of gardenias. She handed it to her.

The windows of her room faced the sea. She looked out elated, aroused by the beauty all around her. In a courtyard across the way, a canary hung in a bright green cage. The courtyard was festooned with flowers — gardenias, roses, carnations, an espalier of heavenly blue morning glory.

She turned, her eyes travelling over the intricately carved chest, the massive handpainted headboard, the beautiful marble table. Charming, she thought, absolutely charming.

Stretching out on a cotton coverlet that smelled of fresh air and sunshine, she hugged herself with happiness. She closed her eyes. Like a genie he reappeared, swinging down from the carriage, his heel springing lightly from the stone quay. She lingered over his buttocks, his thighs, his long, broad back.

She awoke refreshed from her sleep, showered and dressed, made her way down to the cafes, passing a park along the way where several women stood conversing in the shadow of the tall pines while their children played nearby. They seemed as remote as if she were viewing them from another point in time, another planet. Did he belong to one of them?

In a cafe with a clear view of the harbor she sipped ouzo and sampled a plate of hors d'oeuvres. The cafe hummed with the murmurings of foreign tongues. Next to Georgianna a couple conversed in French, behind her a party of Italians. Hand-embroidered smocks, beautifully fashioned silver and gold jewelry, displays of Bain de Soleil beckoned from shops along the harbor. She kept an eye on the sea avenue that ended below the cafes. At intervals a carriage returning with its tourists swept into view.

His was the fourth to appear. The passenger seat was empty. The rush of harness and bell sent a thrill through her. He spotted her as he passed below, his horses slowing to a canter. His eye caught her up, held her in a lightning flash. She trembled. He was gone in a clattering of hooves. She waited, hoping he would reappear on foot, seek her out in the archipelago of tables.

She became engrossed in the scene around her. The waiters moved with the dexterity of dancers, wielding their trays like shields. Their uniforms were crisp. Her waiter had a hawk nose, broad cheeks, eyes so clear she was set to musing. He was immaculate, his hair perfectly groomed. He set her drink before her with elegant restraint.

She turned to the water. A charter boat was tying up at the dock. She watched the passengers step out. How foolish of me to think he'd come, she chided. I'm behaving like a schoolgirl. The sun was a conflagration in the windows of the hotels. The sea had transformed into mother of pearl.

She followed the avenue to a restaurant whose balcony was dotted with lanterns and jutted out over the water. A young many appeared out of a side street, falling in step beside her. "Kanome parea?" he murmured. She averted her face, drew away from him. What do those words mean? she thought, wishing the carriage driver had come to the cafe.

Will I see him again, she mused? She imagined riding into the night beside him, the creaking of harness, the wind whipping her hair, the trees eclipsed by flying hooves. A spasm of emotion closed her throat, leaving an ache in her breast.

When she reached the balcony, dinner was in full swing. A dark eyed boy appeared at her table with a tray. He set water, bread, silverware out on the linen cloth. He stopped and looked at her as if she were something rare, with the same clear gaze she'd observed in the hawk-nosed waiter, the same dignity of bearing.

"Thank you," she said, with a smile, wishing as she

spoke that she'd brought her phrase book.

She glanced out over the water. The stars were beginning to flicker. All around her conversation, laughter, the fragrance of lamb, olive oil, spices, the clink of glass.

Restless and disturbed, as if something were waiting for her under those stars, she left her meal half eaten and moved out into the night. The air was fragrant with blossoms, the moon incandescent. In the lambent waters, a ferry boat strung with lights floated the horizon like a gigantic wedding cake. She found a point of land with an unoccupied bench facing the water. A zephyr caressed her face and her bare shoulders. She sat for a long time, listening to the lapping of waters on the rocks below, the murmurings of passersby. Behind her a bazouki was playing. Wisps of laughter drifted in and out on the breeze. The air was mild. Still she shivered, drew her shawl around her. She stood and began to move towards the music.

In the velvet black of an upper street, he appeared, an apparition blinked from the eye of night. He was with another man, stopping before her, lowering his head. His eyes caressed her face, her neck, her breasts, laying a subtle claim to her. He smiled, his eyes heavy. "Kaly speda," he whispered, huskily. She nodded. His friend had fallen back a step. His eyes continued to caress her. He inclined his head quietly, moving on, disappearing into the dark.

She began to tremble. She heard voices in song, people emerging from the trees. Three men, elbows linked, followed by two women. One of the men called out to her. He gestured for her to join them, turning to her as she passed, with puckered lips. His companions laughed. One of the women wagged her head at him.

Georgianna wandered to her room with an aching heart. To be so near and not be able to speak to him. There was much she needed to know, so little time. She slipped free of her clothes, stretched out in a langour of desire. She imagined his quiet eyes moving over her naked body, his hands on her. She touched her finger to her vulva. It was dripping. Her fingers slipped in, pressed to the throbbing point. She came in a rush, almost at once, with a startled laugh. She twisted her body on the cool sheets, her longing for him unslaked.

She slept restlessly, waking with a start. The sun cut blades through the shutters. She put on her white bikini, wrapped her hips in a cotton skirt. She felt deliciously free, the night a phantom that had flown. She flung open the shutters. Light flooded the room. She stretched high, feeling the pleasant pull of her breasts, touching her fingers to the sloping sides.

She swung out the door, flipping her beach bag over her shoulder, headed for a steaming cup of coffee, lazy morning postcards, then a hike to a beach on the outskirts of town.

She was halfway to the sand, on an avenue of trees that rang with the dry chorus of cicadas when she was overtaken. She stepped off the road, glanced back over her shoulder. Her heart jumped. He was a titan above her, drawing in the reins. Her heart began to pound. He secured the reins and swung down to the ground.

It was minute before he spoke. "Elate," he said, at last, softly, gesturing to the seat. Her heart was a crescendo. He was so beautiful. He waited, his eyes gentle, flecked with sunlight. He held out his hand to her. She looked at him, helpless to deny, reassured by his quiet. Dropping her eyes, she set her foot to the carriage step. At the touch of her toe to the metal, his powerful hands were on her waist lifting her. She slipped into the seat dizzy from his touch.

He drove straight to the beach. They didn't speak, communicating through sidelong glances. When he lifted her down he held her for a moment. Her breasts brushed his chest. She inhaled his male scent. When he released her, she was weak in the knees. He held out his wrist and pointed to the six on his watch, then to the town behind them. He gestured as if he were lifting a cup to his lips. "Yes," she said, "six o'clock." He turned regaining his seat with the movements of an athlete, wheeling the horses, his eyes riveted to her in a parting look.

She swam a quarter of mile, around a barrier of rock, to a stretch of sand inaccessible from the road. Discarding her suit, she shifted to her back in the water, buoyed by the salt, offering her face and breasts to the sun, letting her legs hang loose. Her driver rose from the waters naked, Poseidon in a chariot of gold, his eyes bright emeralds, seaweed streaming from his loins. The waves wantonly plied the lips of her vulva.

In the long, hot afternoon, she paced the upper town restlessly, visiting the local museum, soberly noting the sealed box of Bouboulina's bones. Life had never seemed more precious, its loss more unacceptable.

The heat draped her flesh like gauze. Her room was close and dark. The landlady had closed up the shutters, taken some of her perfume. When her surprise passed, she sensed a justice at work. If it was jealousy, it was deserved. She'd never felt so feminine, so alive. It was worth a dozen careers. She stepped into the open air shower across the hall, a well flooded with sun. She turned her face up to the cooling spray. She stood for a long time, letting the water run down her spine, her buttocks, between her thighs, in a confusion of sensation and dream. She perfumed her thighs, her ears, the soft joints of her arms. At the cafes, she took a table where she would be easy to find.

At 6:20 he hadn't shown. She was beginning to be alarmed. Had she understood him? She considered leaving her seat, walking to the quay where the carriages were. Her courage failed her.

At 6:35 his head appeared, at the far end of the

esplanade. He was with the friend of the night before, a slender man his age, in his early thirties perhaps.

"Signome," he said to her with feeling, his eyes sad with apology. "Dimitry," he offered, introducing his friend.

"Please excuse us," said Dimitrius.

She said nothing, filled with the sudden joy of his presence.

"I was unable to come sooner, and my friend has need of a translator. He wishes to ask if you will go with him to watch the sunset."

She turned her eyes to the carriage driver. He was probing her face anxiously. "Christos," he said to her, pointing his finger to his chest.

His name fell like a petal from his lips.

"Tell him yes," she answered. "Tell him I'd like that." She tried to hold her voice steady. She had scarcely the breath to talk. His eyes never left her face. She felt oppressed by the rich weight of his body. She turned to his friend, to regain her bearings.

"Christos what?" she asked.

"Iannopoulos," he replied. "I am Dimitrius Ritsos, at your service."

Christos attended to the foreign words, his eyes suffused with light. He turned to her, his face bright with happiness. She was disarmed by the acuteness of his responses.

"He will take you to a very fine place in the old harbor. And tomorrow, when he has more time, he would like to show you a restaurant that specializes in fish. He would like to take you there, if it pleases you to go. The old harbor is the best place to see the sunset."

"Where is he from? Is he from here?" she asked, without taking her eyes from Christos for an instant, responding to each vibration that passed through him.

"Arcadia," he answered, as if it were the most natural thing that they should both be ignoring him.

"Yes," she said, not knowing any more what she was saying, in her growing knowledge that she would go with him anywhere, if he would keep looking at her that way, never take those eyes away. She longed to reach out and touch his mouth, his chin, to stroke his untamed brows with her fingers, to explore the secret places behind his earlobes, the nape of his neck where the hair lay thick. She was half drunk from his scent. She closed her eyes.

"If you will excuse me," said Dimitrius. "I will be going."

She barely heard. He rose. "Please," she said. "Don't go." She floundered with embarrassment.

His eyes were admiring. He turned and said something to his friend. Christos moved his head in gentle agreement.

"You will tell me more about him, won't you?" she asked, opportunity slipping through her fingers. At hearing the question in her voice, Christos took hold of his friend's arm, quickened with concern.

Georgianna felt a calm steal through her. What more did she need to know? She was beginning to understand why the Greeks were fatalists.

They watched the setting of the sun from the amphitheatre of the old harbor. She found herself being drawn by him into an elaborate dance. He moved loose and large beside her, as they paced the sea walk to the boats, passing the shadowy hulls of ships under construction.

They did not speak, or touch. His face was turned outward to the horizon, receiving the benediction of the light. She understood that it was for this they had come, a gift he wanted to give her. In a stolen glance, she memorized his profile, basked in the luminosity of his eyes. She sighed.

He turned to her, with questioning eyes.

"What I would give to kiss your lips?" she said. "With you I feel no shame." The sight of his puzzlement made her playful, but she didn't dare put her hand out to touch him.

He drove her to the cafes, parked the carriage, walked with her to where they had rendezvoused. Her landlady's son, Nikos, was standing to the side of the cafe. If he saw her coming, he gave no sign. She was cheered by his sturdy figure, already feeling the emptiness that would follow when Christos left her, the impatience she had brought from her other life threatening to spoil her moments with him.

He conveyed through signs that he would come for her at eight o'clock the next evening, pointing to the cafe. The hawk-nosed waiter passed, his tray high, throwing a glance to Christos.

With an abandon born of her sorrow at parting, she gazed up at the man she would have for her lover. Her look spoke plainly of her desire. He received it, held for an instant, his eyes brimming. His lips parted barely, the merest hint of a kiss. He turned, moving into the throng. She felt suddenly bereft. She looked around her. Nikos remained at his post. She went to him, smiling. He glanced down at his feet.

"Will you come have dinner with me?" she asked, in her most encouraging tone.

"Then katalaveno," he replied, shifting his stance.

"I know. I know." She put her fingers to her mouth, rubbed her hand in a circle over her belly, reached out to take his hand, as if she would lead him. He drew back, stiffened his neck at the impropriety, glancing around to find if anyone had seen. He considered her for a time. With a motion of assent he took a step ahead. She had in mind a popular restaurant at the upper end of the quai, but he motioned her to follow. They entered a dark street, the lights behind them suddenly eclipsed. Overhead a cloud of stars converged. As they climbed, the street narrowed to a lane, the walls of the houses close enough to touch on both sides. Near the top of the hill, he turned into a street black but for a light bulb in a distant wall in whose glow a handful of scattered tables stood revealed. They took a table under the light. The walk had helped release her pent longing, had drawn her deeper into the mystery of the island with every turn of wall, as if the town were a language she were learning with her body.

The menu was a heiroglyph. She shrugged bewildered. He took command, as if he had been raised to it.

He gave the order to the girl, a daughter perhaps, his teeth flashing.

The food was simply prepared. Pork and greens cooked together somehow with lemon, the flavor out of this world.

Nikos refused the meat, would touch nothing but the potatoes. Another mystery. How stern he is, she thought, how manly. Images of Christos chased through her mind.

Overhead a star fell, tracing a bright trail. In her eyes, the sighing of winds. On the hilltop high above, a graveyard adorned with marble coffins on which bouquets of flowers, tiny bottles of olive oil, charms and crosses, cups and other household gifts had been laid, as if death were an interruption merely in an enduring complicity.

He was late again. She considered her impatience, the whirring wings of her internal clock. Time was altogether different for him, not a thing he was rushing to catch, but a companion by his side, moving in harmony. She was determined to acquire that rhythm, to carry it back with her. She closed her eyes.

When she opened them, he was coming toward her. Again, she thrilled to the sight of him. He was carrying a camelia. He handed it to her, with an awkwardness that suggested he was as overwhelmed as she.

They rode to the old harbor to a restaurant in a grove of trees, barely visible from the road. The plaster walls were unadorned. Some workmen were seated at a table by one of the two windows. Dimitrius was with them. He made a sign to them with his eyes, the barest tremor of greeting. She felt a rush of relief to see him there. He could explain to Christos. They moved through the restaurant to a table outside under a trellis burdened with grape vines. The table was covered with oilcloth, dimly lit.

She pointed to Dimitrius, made a beckoning sign to Christos. Dimitrius came at once.

"Please tell him" she urged with pain, "I have to leave in the morning." Dimitrius looked at her uncomprehending. "It's true," she said. He looked at his friend. His eyes were sad.

At the news, Christos withdrew deep into himself, emerging after what seemed an eternity to reach out and lay his warm hands on her arms resting on the table. Her hands were tightly clasped, her expression dolorous.

As if it were a weight he were throwing off, he shook his head and gazed at her, his eyes shining with purpose.

He left her and going inside drew Dimitrius aside. Dimitrius nodded as he listened, his eyes low.

As they left the restaurant, Christos' arm circled her waist, his fingers pressing into her. Under the trees, his lips found hers. He kissed her eyes, her temples, the lobes of her ears. "Agape mou," he said, kissing her lips again. Sweeping her into his arms, he carried her under the moon to the carriage, setting her down, pressing her to him. She felt the full length of his sex against hers. She was half in a swoon, scarcely aware that he was taking the blanket from the seat, drawing her with him toward the water where a rowboat waited. He helped her in, pushed off with an oar. With long, powerful strokes he maneuvered the boat out into the deep, setting a course parallel to the shore. Above the cliffs a forest of pines embraced the sky. He rowed with close attention to his work, as if he were listening for something. From time to time his eyes caressed her. She was rigid with excitement, mesmerized by the motions of his body. She longed to see him naked, to wed her flesh to his. She loosened her grip on the boat, closed her eyes, turned her face up to receive the moon.

In a cove, backed by a towering cliff, on a lip of white sand, he spread the blanket, drawing her down beside him, touching her cheeks, her lips, her nipples erect with excitement. He kissed them each swiftly through the cloth—her stomach, her crown of venus. Together they released her from clothing. Her naked body was iridescent on the dark blanket. Her blind fingers were working his pants free as he held her half raised. She was rocked by spasms of sensation. Her legs fell open. He filled his mouth with her breasts, each one in turn, as if he'd rehearsed the act in his mind. His tongue encircled her nipples. Taking hold of her hips and lifting them, he sought the nectar that dripped from her. She reached for his cock, grasping the silken casing which slipped through her fingers over a core of steel.

His tongue on her clitoris aroused her to a frenzy. When she came he shuddered with ecstasy pressing his mouth into her, moving up swiftly to her face. His mouth was on hers, his cock sliding in full, a joining so total she held him fast, wanting to hold with him forever inside her, to feel the tip of his cock, pressed forever to her womb, eternally charged with its cloud of life, eternally thrusting.

He took her through a series of crescendos, the final mounting to a peak that drained her shoulders, her arms, her forehead. The cloud swirled up inside her. He rocked her in his arms. She wept, pressing her wet cheek to his.

He fell asleep with his face on her breast. She was brimming with light, preternaturally wakeful, unwilling to sacrifice the night to sleep. She drifted in and out of slumber, waking each time to the imprint of his cheek, running her fingers through the coarse silk of his hair, pressing his cock to her belly, her thigh, holding it.

With the first light he stirred, drawing her to him by instinct, his cock finding the opening uninstructed.

They rode back to the harbor, in silent sympathy. The pines had flown, the grove. His eyes were calm.

At the cafes, the waiters lounged in a loose gathering of chairs. The hawk-nosed waiter was not among them. They climbed the street to her room. She drew him inside. He followed intent. She searched her purse for a pen. "Your address," she said, "your phone." It seemed unimportant to him. He touched her cheek, his eyes gracing her forehead. His eyes seemed to be reassuring her, to hold a promise. She knew she would have to part from him now, not at the boat. She couldn't part from him at the boat.

On the plane going over the North Pole, waking to the wonder of the Northern Lights, she understood that she couldn't go back to what she had been. He would be waiting for her. They hadn't ended.

Sky Come

Charlotte Mendez

The desire she felt for the sky was the same as that she had felt for the dearest men in her life, neither more nor less powerful, neither more nor less sexual. The men had all left, of course, but the sky never did. If its presence was sometimes a kind of absence, still it was always there in its various illuminations. And even when it left its glories, it never left.

If there were a man like that—one who might endlessly assume divinely colorful aspects, surprising, wondrous, which like the sky's might come and then leave her, and yet would never fully be an absence; might sometimes put on a dove-gray sobriety and starless black, but would still be sky or man or lover.

To herself she was like that! Did the love of the sky make her realize it? She found herself wonderful in all her illuminations, which like the sky's came and then dissolved, both rapidly and subtly. She wondered if there could be some very small being—some microbe—which paused and saw these glories in her, the way she stopped and saw the sky's: The sun slanting into a gray morning, coloring just the top of the hill across her valley. The pale, fathomless white that slowly gathered meaning in the fall of its snow. The late afternoon of deepening, unutterable blue, with coppery light. And all the magnificent variations of farewell to the sun—the winged, gold-edged clouds, the sweeping strokes of rose and coral and softest apricot, the allure of vermillion clefts—all the illumined passions of declining day. If it was difficult for humans to see that in each other, perhaps the sky itself saw it. Possibly they mirrored one another.

The woman had heard all those myths which assumed that the sky was male and the earth female. However, she did not identify with the earth any more than with the sky, though she loved them both. And though it would be convenient to think of the sky as a male lover, for it called to her so passionately day after day, she felt that more likely the sky was an androgyne. It was surely as soft as it was hard, as female as male, as vaginal as phallic, as....

The thing was, whatever its sex, she had decided to have an affair with the sky. The woman was strangely confident that the sky wanted her, despite all her recent pessimism about love. Perhaps if any man had called to her as deeply as the sky seemed to these autumn days, she would have felt this surging joy with him also. But wasn't this enough, this actual love?

Yes, she said to the sky, I want us to be lovers.

Then come, said the sky. Find a meadowy, high plateau and come to me. My winds are keening for you, I am at midday a kaleidoscope of splintered light, of shattered rainbow for you. Come quickly!

Oh yes, the woman said. Quickly! Don't go away! Oh, wait for me, I'm coming!

She climbed to the top of the nearest mountain range, where a long plateau lay in the form of a sleeping human. There she did some yoga breathing exercises which gently blew soft spaces between all her atoms, until she expanded large enough to be the sky's lover. Actually she did this almost too well, so that she extended beyond the soft plateau into a bumpy area, which was a little uncomfortable.

Never mind, said the sky, a very considerate lover as

it turned out. I will put this sun-warmed cloud under your head and this other beneath your—

Please don't be too skillfull, too sophisticated, the woman said nervously. No fancy Kama Sutra stuff, please—at least at first!

Just wanting you to feel good, said the sky, paling as if slightly hurt, slightly thrown off its style.

The woman laughed at herself. How could she let nerves spoil her trust in the sky? Hadn't they longed for each other, loved each other, for eons?

Never mind, she reassured. I won't be nervous any more.

Once again the wind or passion was sailing through her. She kissed the sky ardently, lingeringly, all along a rosy, mother-of-pearl fissure. Never mind, she said again. I love your cloud pillows, I love you. I ohhhhh Lord, that color, not *that* exquisite color, do you know what it does to me?

Mmmmm, said the sky, and it unfolded the color relentlessly, slid it over the woman's breasts and nuzzled her belly with it. And the color changed so subtly the woman could hardly bear it, so that she moaned softly, oh sky, come

and the sky did come in a gentle time, and so did she, again and again, right into darkness. In the night there was a wild storm, with cracks of light tearing through the darkness, here, there, setting ablaze her ear, the back of a knee, some tiny nerve within her belly, until both she and the sky were nothing but roaring darkness and erratic light. Until at last a calm again, a floating, placeless, intimate silence.

Then the sky gave her stars like the desert stars of the woman's childhood and she floated among them for awhile—for the spaces between her atoms had grown so vast now that she was as big as the universe of stars. Then she looked down for the old sky, her lover, and saw that it was gone. She felt lost and alone among the stars.

Oh I'm so afraid! I'm so afraid! she called out to the stars, which passed right through the spaces between her atoms. They answered together in minor chords, Do not fear, do not fear. But she flew on into the terror of night, even on past the stars, except for those that hovered in her spaces and remained with her.

And she thought, oh my little sky, my little sky with your show of color from a little sun, your tiny clouds like a baby's toy beads, oh my little sky I will never see you again, I've outgrown you, I've gone past you. And you were once so great a lover to me....

It was me, said the universe, said it silently in a voice of unheard music, It was me all along, and you'll never outgrow me.

And blissfully the woman floated with all her own atoms and spaces and all the stars she'd absorbed, right into her beloved.

Mmmmmmmm, said the universe, This time it will never end, for we have swallowed time, Beloved, we have swallowed time and space and our bliss is resounding in the silence, our ecstasy is the circle whose center is everywhere. Oh come and be!

Tahiti

M.M. Roberts

I have this inflatable boat. It's called a Tahiti. It's bright yellow and about twelve feet long, pointed on both ends and two feet wide at the middle.

In it, I want to float naked with my friend along a slow green stretch of silent river, private river, some preserve where other people can't enter and even mosquitoes are banned. The boat is undulant on the dark water, flexing like flesh. The pale gray and turquoise flash of a kingfisher smashes the mirror surface. Feeding trout dimple the glare. Dragonflies hover near us, curious. We cup at the hips, kneeling, straddled. Somehow the boat will be wide enough. We'll both be ready then joined solid, welded at the crux. Her eyes will be as open, as hungry as her body. I will be all the way into her, lost, Odysseus. We drift, turning slow circles. Time disappears. The current quickens. Small waves begin to lick at our fragile craft. The boat pitches, water splashing over the bright sides. Rocks loom and are lost in the swirl. Standing waves toss us into the air then drop us, toss and drop. The roar of the river deafens us. A mist lifts from the surface of the river as we careen toward the waterfall, spinning out of control, flotation tubes thrashing around us like thighs. She paddles against me, straining with her whole body to breast the wave of me. We're beneath the blue-green surface then back into the yellow sunlight, flailing for breath. We plunge through the heart of the torrent, socketed into eternity. The boat bucks and leaps the wave at the base of the big drop. Waves bellow around us. We scream as a solid wall of water slaps us, every cell awake. The Tahiti climbs yellow and glorious into the sunlight.

Below the rapids we drift calmly, soaked. Limp in each other's arms, sagged into each other's body. The boat turns one way and another in the current, sometimes catching up in the eddy behind a big rock and circling there while we sleep, while we chew lazily on each other for sustenance. Skin on skin. Skin on hot yellow plastic. Then the river starts to quicken again. The boat slides forward. She clamps herself on me and starts to paddle. Her eyes shine with boundless life. Whitewater. The torrent taking us forward.

Or maybe we could do it on a lake, in the dark, the Tahiti rocking like an open ocean. Or in the bright yellow boat on the living room floor, imagining the rest. What the heck.

Golden Trout

Pierre Delattre

Seated on the porch of the Town Hall this Saturday night, I looked over my shoulder through the open door just now and, seeing the fiddler jiggling his bow on stage, I had what I guess you'd call a flash of recognition. I saw that our golden girl was caught and had been caught for a long time though none of us has known it, and perhaps she herself doesn't even know.

Perhaps when he realizes he has her on his line he'll let her go so she can belong to all of us again like the muskie we call Brunhilda who trails the flashing lures of many of us fishermen from the edges of her mouth and gills, displaying her jewelry with an impudence that claims the whole of Sleepy Lake as her territory, swimming in plain sight under our piers every now and then before crossing the lake to the dangerous side to wait for us by a fallen log in the shadow of the virgin trees.

There she is, our shell-bejewelled Korrigan whirling away from the outstretched hand of one partner to the arms of another. For all the snowy pallor of her hair and skin, some kind of source energy richer in its connection to the land than any of our transplanted breed could claim suggests that her mother might well have crossed the water to breed with the last Indian still alive somewhere over there in the great forest on the Reservation.

The mystery of her origins makes it all the more intriguing to watch Korrigan dance. Since the first night she walked into the Hall out of the woods some ten years ago not yet quite a woman, she has never missed one of the traditional Saturday nights, though no one ever brings her and no one has yet succeeded in taking her home. Nor have I ever seen her sit out a dance or leave the floor until the final frenzy of the fiddle sends her reeling out the door, across the porch and down the steps into the darkness where she steadies, gives a last shake of her feathered skirt and walks off again down into the woods.

As I looked just now, I finally understood that none of us dancers would ever be the one to take her arm, after the lights go out, to lead her to his car and home to his bed. Just as well to keep the fantasy. She belongs to someone apart. I suffer a little to know she won't be mine, but not very much. After all, I had my chance. She did appear one morning at my cottage on the shore. If I had shown her what she came to see, she might have been moved to love me. But it was a new assignment for a fishing guide, and I grew overly eager. That's all right.

She sat by the fire of my wood burning stove and let me cook her up a meal of fresh greens and corn from my garden. We tipped back in kitchen chairs and she listened intently while I told her what it's like to watch the fish make love. Then she danced with me all through the afternoon, keeping the rhythm with the shaking of rattles and shells at her ankles and wrists.

Since then, I haven't taken my turn dancing with her on these Town Hall nights. I prefer the memory of our last dance there in the little space of my cottage with the table pushed against the wall. I was too shy for the beauty and mystery Korrigan creates around herself to so much as reach out and touch her finger tips. Yet, to tell you the truth, I was more excited and more totally satisfied than I ever have been while making love with a woman, lover that I like to think I am. So I have enjoyed her in my fashion, not just the way most of us men have, as a fantasy; and I'm not really upset, in fact rather pleased to realize she loves someone who has become in the crowd what I have become in solitary — a fisherman through his music.

Yes, he might release her, mightn't he? I can see he's one of those very sensitive young men akin to the ones who like to play their fish more than they like to haul her in. They never let the line go slack, but they don't exert too much pressure either. Such men like to tire their fish. They let her run, reel in, let her run again until she's too exhausted to more than rise weakly nearby, not facing the boat to fight but exposing her vulnerable side just as I saw Korrigan do tonight, between one partner and another, dropping her hands to her sides and facing him with parted legs, looking up to the stage tired and slightly delirious.

Such men never resort to gaff or even net. I have seen the likes of him moved to such contrition that they'll reach quietly into the water, lift her under the belly, remove the hook from her lip and open their hand. The fish lies there for a moment on the submerged palm, tail waving, then slowly drifts down into the deep — almost wanly, you might say.

Or even if such a fisherman claims her, it's not hard to see how sad he feels as she lies on the bottom of the boat with one huge reproachful eye gazing upward. So who knows but what he might realize Korrigan's a special kind of woman, born of the legends we've spun around her, meant to be left free after every dance to walk off back to her hiding place in the woods. Our golden girl.

You won't find the golden *fish* on any of those oval plaques hung on the walls of our dance hall, though I could have caught *her*, at least, if I had wanted to. The biggest muskie on the wall is mine. Bigger than Brunhilda, the one they called Old Siegfried. In this county of lakes, ours is what is called a fisherman's paradise and quite a number of those fish were caught either by me or by men who went out in my boat. This is not to boast, but to tell you a fact: I was the best fishing guide in our neck of the woods from the time I was a boy until a morning a few years ago when I stepped lightly with my fly rod from behind a tree to a slab of rock above the same calm pool of water where, on later visits, I would discover that the fish came for the spawning dance.

Keeping the shadow of the sun behind me, I peered down and saw suspended midway between the surface and the sand a golden trout I knew had been transplanted to our region as a fingerling from the high sierras of California by a wealthy game fisherman experimenting with the adaptation of certain breeds from higher to lower world.

I looked down upon this truly most beautiful fish I'd ever seen in my life and my heart should have quickened with the excitement of wanting to hook it and pull it out of the water. I should have been cunningly thinking of just which fly would do the trick. But neither my body nor my mind reacted in the usual way, perhaps because I dared not move lest the fish flash away and I never get to look at its kind again. Standing on stone, I became stone. I could not leave looking at the fish, neither wanting to take her nor wanting to leave her. The distance between us seemed somehow perfect. Time stopped.

Years have passed and I stand there still. In stillness I stand. Nor does the fish move. We are both suspended; I in the air, the fish in water.

For a long time we were caught in such perfect balance inside my head at the cleavage of my thoughts that nothing swam through my brain. I see now we were at the same distance from the center surface of the pool, both caught on some common connection. The fish just barely stabilized herself with a slow motion of her tail and fins. She divided my emotions down the middle, they fell asunder, and I could neither hear nor feel nor smell nor touch nor taste my surroundings. I was not what I had been, nor yet what I would be. The spine of the fish had severed me from an impulse that dissolved and congealed into a new consciousness forming these words: *So. This is the golden trout.*

Golden. The word was not exaggerated, but I had not realized there would be dots of bright gold on a more brassy color, and that these dots would send out rings that expanded, faded and vanished near the rim of the pool only to seem to quiver from under the over-hanging weeds to form ever more solidly again as they were gathered back through space into the body of the fish like planets blown out and sucked back by the bellows of its gills.

Whether or not these expanding and contracting rings were an illusion, they connected my awakened mind to a reversal I was used to performing with a fisher's skill by turning the surface of the pool upside down, flipping it over so that the fish who thought it was going to rise and, with firm lips, pluck down into its heavier element whatever insect struck that flat boundary between water and air, instead would be snatched into the lighter element I breathed. The surface didn't simply flip over but kept turning all the way back to its origin. I was in some sense the fish and the fish was me, and we were both caught by such surprise that laughter rippled up and blew out bubbling from my mouth and the trout, with a friendly rise, broke the mirror with its tail and shot into darkness.

What had made such sense all these years made equal nonsense. Just like that, it seemed incomprehensible to me that I had devoted so much of my life to catching fish. Why had I wanted to pull these creatures from the places where they so obviously belonged? I didn't even like their taste.

I threw my pole into the bushes, dove into the pool and floated on my back, kicking my feet slowly, balanced with hands out flat at my sides. I watched a flight of geese pass over, felt immensely happy. I left my tackle box there on the shore and have never had the slightest inclination to take a fish out of water since, though I enjoy watching the contentment of others when they sit in their boats holding a pole, head cocked, gazing at the shore, and I love the excitement of the children when they proudly hold up their catch on a stringer as their boat passes my cottage.

The way grown men hold up a ruler alongside their fish to show how many inches they got is something else again. The aspect of sexual lust in fishing intrigues and disturbs me more and more. I look out my window sometimes at a boat anchored up the lake: the poignancy of our persistent yearning to make this no longer very appropriate connection to the watery world of origins. This yearning for the mystery that causes men to cast out and stare at the woods while their lure sinks and they wait for a message from elsewhere, a signal from the depths supposed to strike this wiggling piece of plastic from a bait shop.

Holding the pole at alert between their legs, they wait for the tip to shudder, and I have seen otherwise calm men go into strangely sexual convulsions as the rod bends and they reel in, mouth open, breath blocked at the throat, sometimes an involuntary gagging sound.

The advent of the spinning reel with its hole at the center of the cone out of which the transparent monofilament line is pulled out like the first pure drop of a man's arousal stretched between his fingers; and the sexiness of the lures, some even with frayed skirts (the jigs) increases the erotic suggestion, at least for me; and I know we tend to project our own perverse visions on the innocence of others, so I must confess here a personal experience that may have distorted my vision. A

woman, whose occasional lover I was, ended up in the
hospital as a consequence of trying to protect herself
from my seed (and the seed of others). She had bled pro-
fusely from a device hooked into the cervix to cause her
to abort should she start a pregnancy. Assuring me that
it would be safe to visit her, she had shown me this
I.U.D. before she took it to the clinic for insertion and
we had laughed merrily over the way it resembled
nothing so much as one of my three-pronged fishing
lures, even with a length of nylon leader hanging down.
This leader turned out to serve as a wick that caused an
infection leading to curettage and great loss of blood.
So much for confession. I can't expect everyone else to
make the same associations, either, when the iron head
of the stringer is pushed through the mouth out the gill
and the captive is tossed overboard to be dragged
behind in the classic position of the slave. Can I?

Mine is not a moral position, simply an experience
that remains full of contradiction since I now love the
taste of fish and eat the catch of others with relish after
I've buttered it and baked it, spread it with bits of
sauteed garlic, a lime squeezed over the browned skin.
Delicious.

One morning of my late teenhood, I shipped oars
and lay them down softly, and slowly raised a finger to
my lips to signal the overweight, white faced, pugnosed
man from Chicago who sat in the back seat looking still
a bit dazed from eleven and a half months in a noisy fac-
tory. We were coasting now along the shore of the Indian Reservation, closer than most men dared go, under
the hoary branches of spruce, the creaking arbor vitae,
with a rush of sweet humus and lichen exhaled from the
boulders between which fallen logs lay like crocodiles,
water sloshing into jaws that remained forever agape in
the shallows.

My client hadn't heard the rumors yet about men being caught in snares that trailed from these overhead

limbs. Fishermen had been found hanging upside down, their heads bobbing in and out of the water, the fish nibbling around their nostrils, minnows poking their heads into their open mouths. My client only knew the Reservation was forbidden territory. He had been a bit wary when I turned our boat away from the opposite shore and told him we were going to row across to where the fierce fighters could be found. He glanced nostalgically across the mile of water at the dusky hunting and fishing lodges amongst small, safe stands of tame trees, the tourist cabins with smoke already curling from their chimneys, the barns and farmhouses and hayfields on the hills. He sat there with bulging eyes as he looked at me now for reassurance, gripped the sides of the boat, blinked away the wetness, but grinned like an excited child all the same while I, with the calm assurance of my know-it-all early manhood, nodded to let him know this was the spot all right. Here is where I promised him, if the bats didn't spook him when they began to swoop ("Hell, no."), nor the sight of a bear trundling out of the woods into the lake to stand like a comrade a few feet from our boat until he had fished up a bass with his paw and carried it back to his family and the fish he'd dispersed returned to their haunts, Old Siegfried especially to lie alongside his twin log ("A bear catch a fish, hunh? That I'd like to see")…here is where Old Siegfried was going to be lured out from that log, the hugest, oldest, wiliest muskie in all of SawSaw County ("No shit!"). The muskie who liked to disguise himself as that log you see right over there where the golden birch leans.

Here was a man accustomed to street lights when he was out of doors, willing to row home in darkness even if his wife would be a little worried, since it was six miles up the shore after we'd rowed back across. So ready was he to do battle, I could see his Adam's apple bob in his throat like a float when a bass tugs hard at the line.

The lichened trees leaning over boulders with menacing brows, roots snaking across the rotted forest floor, trees much larger than you were accustomed to shouldering up to in these parts, with a fetid breath exhaled from their wounds and with eyes inside those purplish holes, bird or animal or...what? He had heard about the little wild girl Korrigan whose crazy mother let her swim naked across the lake to run with the wild animals. That was one myth about Sleepy Lake that had reached as far as the taverns of Chicago. ("Aw, Mr. Potts, the woman has no daughter I've ever seen, let alone a wild one.")

But we both looked for her and saw eyes in the leaves too, in the ferns, eyes perhaps of animals yet unnamed, uncaught. There is that feeling along the shore of the Reservation, especially when the last cold rush of an expiring day presses over the as-yet warm water, and the bats now start to swoop close enough so that the stories about them tangling in your hair make you grateful you're wearing a hat and remind you with admiration of the infallible soning devices (they *are* infallible, aren't they?) in, what is it, their noses? their ears....On the tips of their devilish wings? Wowee! That one missed me by an inch, the big eyes of my client say. And what is this eerie mist that swirls past us?

He watches me sit there facing him after I've lowered the anchor, waiting for the fish to accept our boat. The laughter of a loon higher up the lake sends a visible chill through his spine. I open my bait box and select the artificial lure he will use. A Heddon white and red, yellow-eyed sexy Go Deeper River Runt with three-pronged hooks at tail and belly. I reach down and slip her to him and make sign language to show how I want him to attach her to his swivel and cast out gently, not reeling in, but as I told him on the way over, just letting her sink sultrily, wiggling toward the bottom, there to lie in the murk a good long time so that Old Siegfried, wondering what she thinks she's doing, too unaroused yet to pursue but eyeing her all the same in case she should have the impudence to rise and expose herself again, begins to imagine the taste of her on his hard, raspy old pointed tongue.

Old Siegfried will ponder the flashy creature with the silver spoon in her mouth and his ornery peasant rage will stir. If you wait long enough so he begins to wonder what she's groveling in the sand about, and only then bring her timidly upward, reeling ever so slowly, as if the little lost River Runt realized she had somehow swum into an ocean of monsters and were glancing about like the woman from the St. Paul Pioneer Press who blithely sauntered alone into the Reservation to interview the last living Indian of that forest's tribe and was never seen again...if you reel her with a sudden dash and then pause, making her appear to shrug as she thinks, oh, what am I worried about, this is a friendly ocean, a safe enough place for a cute little girl with a bright red cape and a pretty white skirt whom everybody dotes on, then Old Siegfried is going to rouse his loglike self. And then....and then!

My client had cast his lure and was waiting for my signal to reel in as he glanced toward the forest, ducking involuntarily every time a bat swooped. The Big Bear could already be seen constellated above us. A dog I knew to be the Indian's Great Dane, howled from deep inside the Reservation. Suddenly my man, who had drawn his head down into his shoulders, stretched his neck out. His mouth fell open. He signaled me with his chin to look over my shoulder at the log where I had said Old Siegfried was hiding. I placed the flat of my hand gingerly over the seat, hoisted myself around to see better. Through the silence I had so insisted upon, his voice was a mere passage of fog.

"What's that?"

"A muskrat," I whispered, uncertain. What I had

seen appear from behind the log was a blond mass of fur. We watched it move out to deeper water, go under, surface.

"Ain't no muskrat."

I turned too late to shush him. But whatever it was didn't seem to hear. We saw now what could be nothing but a head of human hair foraging in the manner of muskrats or beavers, though I'd never seen a beaver along this long stretch of forested shore. The creature now revealed something like a body, a white fluttering length just discernible under the black-green wavy water. It swam still farther out, trailing a molten V, then around and back behind the log.

We thought it had disappeared for good. We were about to break our silence when it stood so that its naked presence was exposed from the waist up. A child faced us, perhaps short-sighted because oblivious to our presence. There was still enough light so that we could see the wiggling creature she lifted to her mouth. As I strained my eyes, hoping she wasn't about to eat our lure, I saw she had a crayfish in her fingers. She pushed it between her teeth and bit down. We could hear the crunch of the shell. She took hold of the claws which stuck up from the corners of her mouth like the tips of a false mustache and was about to twist them off when she too froze.

The boat gently rocked under us. The bats zoomed close to our ears. The chip-chip-chip of two squabbling creatures on the shore, the musky smell blown in from where toads croaked and insects thrummed, the sudden rustle of poplar leaves; but not a movement, not a sound from the little girl in the water or from the awestruck young man I was, nor from him who sat on the back seat, eyes, nostrils, ears and anus wide open. Then she, Korrigan, this myth who really lived, whom I would really be able to say I had seen, with witness to prove it...she broke the water.

There was a splashing, a leap onto the bank, a nudeness that vanished between two stumps as she dropped to all fours and scurried through the ferns. I lunged for the anchor rope, jerked it up hand over hand as it poured water into my shoes, and threw it down so hard it cracked the front seat. I jumped for those oars and I began to tug like we were mired in molasses, nearly ripped my arms out of their sockets, making noises in my throat I would be embarrassed to imitate. I finally tore us loose. We broke and flew over the water, pursued by a rush of icy wind.

One morning, years later, I was seated at my kitchen table with a few maple logs crackling in the stove, my hands wrapped around a mug of hot coffee, when shaking the sleep from my head I glimpsed out the window for an instant the image of Korrigan standing in a cloud of white butterflies beyond my freshly hoed little vegetable garden. I fixed my eyes on the steaming brown murk in my cup, reluctant to look again, for when you live alone a great deal there is always the fear that a tendency towards hallucination will get the better of you and your separation from the ordinary world will be irretrievably lost in fantasies solidified into what is conventionally called madness. I was not yet ready to become the crazy coot some people had started calling me since I quit teaching them how to catch fish.

So I muttered a few facts to myself about the date and the current wars and the coldness in my toes, took a big swallow of the hot brew, breathed deeply and, confident that my illusion had now dissolved, looked again. But there she was, quite real, I decided with a flutter of my freshly caffeinated heart. Quite strikingly substantial. She stood there some thirty feet away, her blond hair curling down the front of her blue shirt which hung over brown pants bloused into rubber boots. She looked like she was ready to be taken out on the lake. Later, when I reflected on our adventure, the word for her that always came to mind was the one used in reference to female fish when they are ready to spawn: *gravid.*

Gravid she stood in front of my cottage with little jewels flashing from the spume of the slugs who had spent the night creeping up and down the grasses. The first dry spot of morning was my patch of garden, and the butterflies liked to warm themselves there on the bare ground. No longer startled by her, they had settled back down and were slowly wafting their wings at her feet. While I had heard that Korrigan occasionally dropped in on people during her ambles through the woods, this had never happened to me before and it seemed clearly a telepathic response to the music I had made. Could I have captured her heart in some mysterious way? The notion started me shaking in an unmanly way. It's terrifying when the gods call our bluff.

I gave a signal to approach, then scrambled about the room grabbing up socks and underwear and a girlie magazine and stuffed them in a drawer, pulled some pants over my longjohns and rushed to the door.

Gravid her voice, too, as she finally spoke to me. She said she had heard that I knew of a place where you could go to watch the fish make love.

I gulped and shrugged. I still hadn't opened the screen door. I didn't want her to see how my knees were shivering. "I must have made such a claim when I was drunk."

She opened the screen door and looked at me with a sober and very touching seriousness that at once made her human and calmed me. "But *do* you know of such a place?"

"In the forest, up Charlie's Creek," I nodded.

"Take me there."

To watch the fish make love, you have to approach the pool like the movement of a moon shadow. Seat yourself on the overlooking rock ledge at least half an hour before dawn while the evening star is still bright in the eastern sky. Become the motionless stump of a tree rooted in the seams of the rock.

If you let your feet dangle, the heads of frog, snake and turtle that surface to peer out at you from their stations in the weeds will submerge with a sudden popping sound that alerts the fish. Double up your blanket and sit upon it cross-legged, folding it over your knees. Wear a loose jacket so your breathing can't be seen. Keep the breaths regular with no rise and fall of the shoulders or chest, no sound from the nostrils.

As the shadows withdraw into the trees and the line of sunlight edges across the pool, you'll see ever more clearly until the bubbles that rise on the column of water at the center will seem to float up and burst on thin air. Sometimes the first warm breath of morning blown down the stream will create wispy vapors, but by the time the first scouts dart into the theatre and start to circle the actors will be as visible as if they were in a well-lit amphitheatre.

Once the scouts see the arena's safe for the ritual, they flit back upstream to notify the others. The gravid female darts out, stops suddenly on the column of water and starts fanning her tail. Then the males appear full speed in a group charge toward her—perhaps thirty of them. She flies upstream, and they pursue. But soon she's back in the pool slowly twisting and turning and flashing her scales as the males, in a pack behind her, take turns trying to keep their nose exactly at her tail. Enough of this sniffing! She starts to roll, showing them her swollen belly. The males go crazy. Furiously they circle faster and faster around her, making the column on which she rests lift her almost to the surface. They dart at her and at each other with such a frenzy now that only she can be seen. The males are streaks of silver, accelerating molecules that set the water to boiling. The frothing surface churns up miniature waves that slap against the sticks on shore. There's an explosion at the center, a high whirling spray and she, too, vanishes in the fury.

You'll be tempted to spoil the performance by gasping or leaning forward; but, if you can keep still, what you'll see with the gradual calming of the waters will be a marvelous image of two fish side by side quivering in tremendous states of excitement. All the others are gone.

How she chose her sire, I don't know any more than I know what it is that gives a certain sperm cell its power over so many others to penetrate the egg. I have often wondered, as I looked at the couple side by side trembling in their ecstasy, how the others knew so suddenly. When they were all in the ring together, the males had darted at each other, often making themselves vulnerable by exposing their sides as if in contempt of attack; but none had actually touched and it seemed doubtful that the victory was so much of strength as of another more thrilling quality: the beauty of the chase, I like to think. An aesthetic victory of imaginative grace, the superlative energy of his aquatic dancing. Yes, it must be imagination and not raw power that prevails. He who sent the most rapturous gestures of fin and tail, the most ardent waves flowing out from his sides to hers was allowed to strike her swollen womb to its bursting.

I remember a poem I once read by D.H. Lawrence in which he compares the frigidity of Christ and the fish because neither makes physical contact with his love. How wrong! What more subtle way to touch than by making waves? Isn't our sensitivity to the waves that flow over and through us and past us from every corner of the cosmic pool the measure of our capacity to respond sensually to Creation? Such high-falutin' mystical thoughts are quite ordinary when one is seated on a rock at dawn shivering slightly, legs tingling from lack of blood for having been crossed so long, gazing down as one waits for the sun to touch the water and the vision to appear.

And there they are for the second act now: she and her lover, tails ashudder, fins vibrating, the electric lines through their spines struck simultaneously and there is a bursting at precisely the same instant. The eggs flower from her womb, his milk spreads an invisible cloud around them. Lifting fast on the water column, the lovers veer apart and shoot off in different directions; she, out of the pool and down to the lake, he, back up against the current to its source.

Only the eggs wrapped in milky sperm remain. The sticky sperm helps them cling to the weeds and stones.

Here I sit on the porch of the Town Hall, and I think I see more clearly as the last dance approaches and the fiddling becomes more frantic, the dance floor more congested. None of us who hope to catch her are going to land her; but he who makes the most beautiful waves, whose imagination creates a new music. Before I took Korrigan to watch the fish make love, she swung her long legs down from the grate alongside my stove and jumped up to dance all afternoon for me, inspired by the instructions I gave her on how we must approach the pool and what we could expect to see. We shook and we quivered and I flattered myself to think she found me the perfect mate, her fisher king. But, as I say, I failed to keep my own advice when later, seated side by side on the rock above the pool in the meadow of the great forest across the lake, we observed the creation. Don't ask me why. Too much excitement, I suppose. No, let's be honest: my pride in being a guide.

Just as I knew they were about to climax, I whispered, "Watch!" Oh, fool that I am.

There is a sad third act we then had to witness. Shortly, he returned from the source and she from the lake and they got to work eating the eggs, wasting no more affection on each other. If the lovers, after the initial relief of having spent all their erotic powers, stop somewhere far apart in a shadowy place to reflect; and if her realizes that in his eagerness he released his milk too soon, or if she remembers that fear caused her to let go too late, if they realize they didn't come at precisely the same instant, they'll know the reproductive energy is bound to have failed, the spawn stimulus will not have achieved its force. And they will return glumly to consume their failure.

Ah, well. It's three o'clock in the morning and we're into Korrigan's Reel, composed especially for her. That fellow she's dancing with may look like a real stud with his pink silk shirt, gold buckle and boots with heels that strike steel against the floor. But I doubt if he has the imagination to synchronize with the likes of her. He's trying too hard.

The fiddler, on the other hand, looks quite at ease. His bow just keeps quivering and shivering over the strings. Chin tucked to his instrument, he watches her calmly over his raised up shoulder. It's for him she dances, yet I can see clearly now that he doesn't want to catch her and that she's not after catching him. They've found the golden distance.

Let the rest of us dart in and out. Some early morning we'll know it's time to withdraw. He'll put down his fiddle and they'll dance alone.

Meanwhile, I'll watch them make waves.

At the Hot Springs During a Meteor Shower

Robert Wrigley

We are made more human here
in the amniotic waters, more alone.
All light is from the moon
unrisen back of Bear Pete Mountain,
and from the tragic stars, stars
alive, stars that die. By tragic
we mean the way the moon,
the solitude of lovers
in the most hospitable waters on the planet,
can make up maudlin, how this is
the dilemma of all who would know
such earthly comforts, while the sky
goes blind with literary pretense,
hokey fakes, the pageantry of adolescence.

We are only human here, only moments
away from gasping, grunting animals,
but far enough to know,
afloat on inner tubes, steaming
in the sudden air of mountain night,
that there are likely no two
in the world so well off as we,
that this happiness of ours,
were it permanent, were it owned .
at some unspeakable price, would be criminal.
This is our confession,
our acceptance of guilt, our sentence:

that tonight it may live in our lives,
in our one commingled memory,
                              and never,
not ever, be forgotten.

In the Dark Pool, Finding You

Robert Wrigley

No lights, no moon, no stars in the mountains,
clouds clearing the night with blackness and an owl
fooling from the pine at the edge of the meadow:
Lover, I am silent moving in these simmering waters,
the sulphur clouds we breathe are invisible
where you taunted with nakedness
and swam away in tease. I am blind.

From his low bough bellows the owl, who sees
you, pink in the earth-cooked pool. I would have
eyes like his if I were dreaming, and a voice
to stir the night with, calling *where? where?*
Instead I am a muskrat, my mop of dark hair
wakelessly moving regimental alleys over the surface
where I will find you and gently gnaw

your shoulder, where your skin will nearly squeak.
These are womb waters, I say aloud, and the owl
goes quiet. I say I am a seed for you,
hoping you'll giggle, hoping somehow the water will
quicken and I'll know what corner you hide in,
what loop you swim around me, what vague dream
the eyes concoct in the lead an owl can live in.

Light is a trick of luck the blind man learns
to live without. Lover, here are my hands
imagining you, all swells and softnesses lightly giving.
In these waters, body-warm, I can make up
where you are, and it will be true.
This is love's skill and power, as real as the owl,
high in the pine, dining on imaginary mice.

Descending Ascent

Sara Donart

Megan lay panting in the musk of the forest floor, her skin damp from flight. Bits of leaf and duff attached themselves to the moist flesh of her arms and thighs, clung to the nape of her neck. She lay on her side, knees bent, rocking from side to side, hugging herself as her breathing slowed.

Eyes already closed, she squeezed them tighter and drew herself into a protected ball, the posture of the yet-to-be-born. Pushing her nose into the sweet decay beneath her, she waited for the rain. The ground was soft, the scent seductive.

Her body, clad in damp t-shirt and shorts, shivered, though the gathering storm hadn't yet cooled the late August afternoon. Beyond the forest shade the air was still warm, the wind just beginning to build, and in the distance thunder tumbled like boulders down the far side of the mountain.

She waited. Relaxed her grip. Remained motionless and willed her mind to do the same. It disobeyed and slipped through bits of the scene just played out down below, down in that mountain meadow in the wide open sun, played out before the thunderheads rolled over the mountains.

It had been a day between two friends, old friends with years gone by between their meetings. Her friend Kathleen lived far from these Rocky Mountains now, far from the clean scent of evergreens and the sharp rock of rising peaks. She had moved east to Chicago, a city dense with people and events, where silence and open space were rare. So for her visit Megan had brought Kathleen here, to country they had known together, where they could walk and talk undistracted, arm swinging, words spilling.

As they climbed high and talked long, Megan appraised the new person in her old friend. Kathleen had a feline assurance now, like the absorbed focus of a cat intent upon a bird. She no longer fumed and raged when speaking with passion, but selected her words precisely, coolly, with an elegant aggression.

Megan studied her as they walked, and when they rested she watched as Kathleen took in long slow gulps of water, head back, eyes closed, neck extended. They sat together on a rock, sharing gorp and water, their arms touching, a study in contrast. Megan was summer-toasted, firm and rounded. Kathleen, dark hair cropped short, glowed white with a sun brush of color on her cheekbones. She looked thinner than Megan remembered, taut and lean. But Megan was most unsettled by her eyes. No longer masked behind the glasses, they gleamed greener and seemed to prowl across the landscape. A direct look was a pounce, and more than once Megan had felt raked by her stare.

After their rest they continued up the trail, falling silent whenever the trail turned steep, breathing in tandem, their footsteps slow. Their destination was a high alpine meadow, tucked above the last lake of the drainage, where summer had only just arrived. After another hour of woods and rock and bursting berry bushes they found their spot, a clutch of color ringed by dun boulders and twisted, hardy pine. Purple shooting star bloomed in thick patches, and the waxy yellow of alpine buttercups lay scattered through the dark mat of meadow grass.

They dumped their daypacks on the soft sunny green and stood silent for a moment, surveying the bare crags of the embracing cirque of mountains. The creek that moved through the meadow was narrow and deep; without a babble or splash it slid silent through the gentle slope of the meadow.

Megan dropped to her stomach and plunged her head into the shock of snow-melt water. When she came up for air, her eyes were open wide, her breathing deep and double time. She watched Kathleen cup her hands and fill them with water. Closing her eyes she brought the water to her face, hands lingering there while the splash turned to little rivers and rivers to tributary droplets, mountain hydrology in backward motion, seeking downward for a source, the reverse of natural order. Megan watched as a rivulet ran from chin to throat, paused at the pool of shadow above Kathleen's breastbone, then continued, a single drop, trickling erratically downward until it slipped from sight beneath the top button of Kathleen's blouse. Megan dove her head into the stream again. When she surfaced her ears burned from the cold. Then she busied herself with their lunch while Kathleen washed.

Megan watched the bathing as she unpacked. First, a crusty loaf of French bread and a small Brie cheese, gone soft and gooey in the heat. Kathleen soaked her scarf in the stream and, head bent, squeezed the scarf over the back of her neck. A jar of creamed herring and two cold artichokes. She dunked the cloth again and drew it slowly up the insides of her arms. Next, a firm avocado, its pebbled skin split in transit, and wild huckleberries, gathered along the way. Kathleen kicked off her shoes and plunged her narrow feet into the water. Finally, a bota skin of red Spanish wine and a single pomegranate. Bending at the waist Kathleen splashed the trail dust from her ankles and, soaking her scarf one last time, dabbed at her thighs as she straightened. The table was set.

Megan offered the bread. Kathleen took it with a look and a grin and joined the assault upon their feast. Hungry hands broke golden bread crusts and tore at the soft yeasty insides. Fingers spread cheese and stripped artichokes leaf by leaf, bared teeth devouring each pocket of flesh. The wine passed. Shirts came off as the sun shone down. Lips turned berry blue. Stretched on their stomachs, lying on their backs, now silly, now serious, they talked of old times and old friends, of lovers they had known and men they had shared.

But at the talk of men and lovers Megan thought she felt her friend cool by a degree, saw her mouth twist wry, the cat creep back. Lying on her stomach now, propped on elbows, Kathleen reached for the lone pomegranate, the last of the feast. Wrapping her long fingers around it, she pierced the skin with her thumb and tore the fruit in two, exposing the chambered seed-flesh inside. She explored the fruit with her fingers, peeling away yellow membrane until each pod stood bare and ruby and ready to eat. She offered half. Megan rolled onto her stomach to reach and accept then felt Kathleen watching her, eating as she ate, red fruit with already blued lips.

Megan dropped a pomegranate seed in the grass and Kathleen reached to rescue it, pinching it with thumb and index and offering it back, an inch out of reach. Megan bridged the distance, stretching her neck and parting her lips to take the seed. Kathleen's finger lingered on Megan's lips, and she told her they were stained purple, did she know? Megan nodded and the finger followed the motion before withdrawing. Then Kathleen lifted the hair that had fallen forward over Megan's face and placed the fist-full of sun-warmed hair on the far side of Megan's neck. Her fingers slipped through the silkiness, twisting the locks to catch the sun, her arm resting, comfortable, across Megan's shoulder.

Megan looked down, avoiding Kathleen's steady green gaze, and then without raising her eyes, she let them wander toward Kathleen and slide along her bare extended torso. Ribs stood in ridge and shadow where skin stretched tight against bone. Her breasts were little more than nippled mounds. Megan thought of the cup her own hand made and thought that, yes, they were that size. The image startled her, and her easiness tensed even before Kathleen pressed her cheek and then her lips against Megan's shoulder.

Leaning against her friend's warm skin, Kathleen sighed deep in her throat, like someone suddenly cozy in the cold dead of winter. But Megan felt her own bones lock, her shoulders tense. Kathleen made no sudden moves, but stroked Megan's back and kept her breathing even. Megan's breath trembled, a reaction to this breach of boundaries, to sensation and confusion. She twisted on her back to face Kathleen, to meet and understand the moment, to ask with her eyes if this lover's touch was meant as such or if the touch was merely friendly and the fantasy hers. In either case her mind met disorder.

Kathleen, in answer, kissed Megan between her breasts, tracing a line downward with her lips, toward the softness of Megan's stomach, suggesting possibility, avoiding the overt. Megan's heart drummed against her breastbone, her skin electric. Kathleen lifted her head, raised her eyebrows and looked at Megan squarely. It was a clear question, a search for a sign, a nod, a shake of the head. But clarity eluded Megan. Thought, emotion and the undeniable body heat she felt spreading down her thighs all demanded center stage, and there they collided. Her body expanded and contracted. Attraction and aversion. There was no answer as simple as the shake or nod of her head. Her answer was flight.

In one motion she was on her feet, her discarded t-shirt in hand, moving across the meadow and away from those things that had no answer. She scrambled up the short slope at the edge of the meadow and slipped into the trees. Regaining the trail there, she stopped long enough to yank on her shirt, pulling it down hard over her nakedness. Then she ran, welcoming the steepness of the trail, the burn in her legs and lungs. She ran until the first rumble of thunder woke her back into an awareness of time and place, reminded her of the lateness of the afternoon, the change in weather and the distance from home. Knees folding, she slumped to the ground, mind again awake to the passage of events. She sought comfort, found relief in the firmness of the un-questioning earth. She thought of her friend, aban-doned below, of the kind of friend Kathleen had been and the kind of friend she could become. Her mind closed again in confusion. She awaited the wash of the storm, longed for an erasure of time, a reversion to the moment before the question was formed, before the question demanded its answer.

When the storm arrived, wind gathering, trees filling with thunder, she unfolded from her fetal crouch and arched her back into the falling rain, cooling her hot skin with each fat drop, staying until the last drop had fallen. And when the storm was past, she gathered herself and left the mountain, wet and weary, treading inevitably downward, purged of nothing.

Rearview Mirror

James Goldsmith

Maybe it was growing up wild in Samoa, maybe it was being the only guy in school with a working knowledge of the clitoris—whatever it was, my man Chris had remarkable luck with the girls.

For the girls, some them anyway, it was like Balboa discovering the Pacific, Newton discovering gravity, or whatsisname discovering LSD. The girl would feel transported, I suppose, lifted into other worlds, hurled into new dimensions, left vulnerable to his smooth, self-serving arguments. If you call two-syllable sentences—Oh, yes!; Let go!; Now, now! Now me!; Touch there!; Faster!; Oh, yes!; Yes, yes!—arguments.

Until he met Jeannie, Chris was a runaround, a shark, and he knew it, with the whitest teeth and most innocent smile, behind which lurked a mind that rose to no loftier heights than a tall girl's tits. The guy had a saying, a motto: even snakes sing in the spring.

Even snakes sing in the spring. Doesn't make a whole lot of sense, but then logic never played even a supporting role in Chris's life. "Do you like it when I touch you like that?" he would say. "Do you want me to stop now?" he would ask. "You know, you can make me feel that way, too," he would conclude. Chris's idea of a syllogism.

Where do I get my information? How do I come by this detailed knowledge? Was this all locker room talk,

Chris a kiss-and-tell kind of guy?

I'd like to say that it was on a double dates, me in the front with my girl, Chris in the back with his. Me hearing what he and she whispered, them hearing what me and my girl murmured. I wish. But such was not the case.

One of my problems is that I'm short, real short. Mom used to say that I was the runt, even though neither sister had more than a couple inches on me.

Another problem is that I'm not attractive — no square chin (actually, no chin whatsoever), no rippling, sinewy calves or big biceps. I'm not ugly, mind you. I'm just not much of anything. When I used to drive down the street in Mom's car, people would notice the car, not me. They never said, "There goes Elbert." They always said, "There goes that red Wildcat convertible."

I'm a smart guy, but that wasn't always a blessing. I got lousy grades in high school, and Dad always said that when I graduated, I'd probably end up back on my old paper route. The couple times I actually had dates during high school, I'd choke and say things like, "So what does your father think about Vietnam?" Or, in an attempt at levity, "On a bet in biology once, I bit off a frog's head." Try to get a kiss after that.

What all this personal information adds up to is why Chris chose me to be his driver that summer when he lost his license. I would pose no threat to him whatsoever — that was probably one factor.

Another was my chameleon-like quality — in May, teachers would still have to ask my name.

But probably it was my unlimited access to Mom's '63 Buick Wildcat convertible. Fire engine red. Bucket seats in front. White leather upholstery.

For me, the arrangement was great, like having the captain of the football team ask me to take him to the Bengals' game; it was an honor.

So I would cruise the countryside around Dayton — out through the gentle fields and forests, top down in sunny and cloudy weather, the tape deck loud enough to mix with the wind blowing past the winged hood ornament, over the waxed red enamel, over the windshield into my hair, around the bucket seats to the back where Chris would be seducing his latest find, gently overcoming any qualms about fooling around in the open convertible, with me up front, feigning obliviousness. I'd have Dusty Springfield or, for romance, The Lettermen going on the eight-track, the rearview mirror elevated, so high, in fact, that all I could see was blue sky, clouds, and the tops of trees.

There were a couple, true, who could never reconcile having me in front while Chris more or less undressed them in back, but there were others who didn't mind, or didn't mind for long, distracted as they were by Chris's stories, accompanied by much kissing and touching.

Chris would relax girls, telling stories — tales, maybe — of growing up on the main island of Samoa. He'd talk about how sexually free everyone was, and how, as a twelve-year-old, he was advanced upon and conquered on sandy beaches.

Always it was outside, often before or during one of the frequent short, heavy rainshowers. How young girls — even girls with only a trace of pubic hair, and tiny little dark-nippled, brown breasts — would undress with him, suck him off, allow him to bring them off with hand or mouth, following it up by a skinny dip in the South Pacific. How they had small, intimate parties on the beaches at night, sex in the black Pacific — tiny, bumping fish, the danger of sharks.

And when his smooth fingers, having somehow slipped inside the girl's panties, stroking the girl's clitoris all the while — well, the results, from my point of view — my driving pillow slipped under me, mirror slightly adjusted — were spectacular.

I guess it somehow comforted girls to know that this guy had seen and done it all, that in his world — and theirs — sex, even sex riding through the wilds of rural Ohio in an open convertible, was as wholesome as ripe mangoes and passion fruit, as squeaky clean as a tropical shower.

I tried using the Samoa stories as my own once on a date, but instead of loosening the girl's inhibitions and clothing, I got off-track and ended up criticizing Margaret Mead's research methods. I took the girl home, at her request, at 9:15.

Those weeks I drove for Chris, I learned a lot about tops. If it unbuttoned in back — forget it, I might as well watch the road. Give me a blouse that unbuttons in front. An unbuttoned blouse always afforded at least a shadowy glimpse of those sweet young breasts, with their soft tan or brown or pink nipples. With pullovers, it was famine or feast. Normally, all I could see was Chris's hand moving under the fabric. Chris might try pulling the pullover up over the girl's breasts, but most felt uncomfortable that way, with their breasts exposed for passing traffic to see, not that there was ever much passing traffic where I drove.

Jeannie, however, favored pullovers, shunned bras, and didn't mind having her breasts out. In fact, it got to where she would bring them out if Chris didn't.

Once we started going out with Jeannie, Chris lost interest in the other girls. For Chris, Jeannie was an empty canvas, a vase ready for flowers, a silver chalice awaiting wine.

Her parents, she said, never spoke about sex, and she didn't learn from friends since she didn't have any. She was never a popular girl, sort of a lonely outcast once she outgrew everyone in the third grade and towered above everyone else. All through school, the image stuck.

It took Chris to discover that without glasses she was sort of attractive, and without clothes she was really, really attractive.

She, too, had just graduated, and she was much more mature than most of our girls. She was built on a generous scale. She didn't have slim hips, and you couldn't even come close to circling her waist with your hands. Her belly was soft, white, and rounded, the world's best pillow, I imagined. Jeannie had wide shoulders like her brother, who had played college football, and she probably could have pounded me, if she had wanted to.

As well as being more mature, she was more fun, calling herself Chris's "main squeeze," Chris her "handyman" and me her "dwarf chauffeur." She'd include me in some of the conversation, even when Chris had her shorts unbuttoned and his hand inside her panties—she'd ask where we were going, how far from the next town we were, did I have a girl, what would happen if we put the top up while we were driving, was I having fun, too.

She met Chris's sexual frankness head-on. If Chris said, "I'll tell you about the last time I masturbated if you'll tell me," she would! And she'd go first!

Whereas other girls had sort of giggled quietly at the little jokes Chris made, Jeannie laughed long and loud, and then joked about how when she laughed, his fingers up inside her, she was really his main squeeze.

Yes, Jeannie was an eager convert to Chris's personal religion—Bless me, dear God, for I...I...think I'm going to come—equally enthusiastic about sex in the convertible. A couple times we parked and they went into the woods, but Jeannie didn't like it—the bugs, the dirt, the stillness and the mysterious sounds. She liked the wind, the car's oceanliner ride, the tape deck. And she said it just wasn't the same without good old Elbert and his good old mirror, kidding me.

If we arrived at her place with the top up, she'd insist we put it down. When we got out to the country and they started fooling around, I'd adjust the mirror, and Jeannie would joke: "Down a little, Elbert. You're only getting the top half," and flash her breasts. The top half was plenty for me, but I'd adjust it anyway, Jeannie in the middle of the back seat, adjusting her knees outward. "Got it, Elbert?" she'd ask, her skirt bunching up around her hips. Generally, I wouldn't — couldn't — reply, my tongue awfully thick and my throat constricted.

And what panties! White cotton, at first, but after a while, more dramatic colors. The day she revealed black panties — the first black panties I'd ever seen on a real girl — I nearly took out a mile marker. And when the panties themselves slid down, there was just white. White skin under black cloth.

And, oh, the way she parted her legs, laying the left against the seat, looping the right over Chris's knee. Chris stroked her a little. After a while, she said, "Oh. Oh, my! Oh, Chris, what are you doing to me?" Shortly, she said, "Oh, this is incredible!" And she said, "Oh, oh, Chris, please, stop. I...I...." And then she said all sorts of things, just little noises, really, but lots of them.

At that point we hit gravel on the left side of the road. We all said something like "Whoa!" as I swerved to the right, dumping the two of them against the left side of the car.

We all laughed. Jeannie didn't seem to mind that I was there, though her laugh was a little shaky. She didn't cover up or anything, even when she looked straight at me in the mirror. And she did look me straight in the mirror, for the longest time.

After the climax Chris helped her achieve, she tried it on her own. There she was, right in the rear seat, legs apart, touching herself as Chris had. But she quit in a minute, telling Chris that she'd need to work on that; she was embarrassed. She said she'd practice that night, right after her piano lesson.

The next day, after she and Chris had petted for a while, she soloed. He held her, encouraging her, telling her to moisten her fingers with saliva. And he helped her, generous soul, lending his own fingers and saliva to the cause. But after a while she didn't need Chris's help. She sort of pushed his fingers aside and began a regular motion, a rhythm, rubbing up-and-down. And then side-to-side. And then up-and-down and side-to-side! Slow for a while, then fast. Two fingers on the free hand dipping inside herself, just so the nails disappeared. She squeezed herself between two fingers, breathing faster, eyes shut, belly heaving, legs quivering, then stopped.

Gradually, she calmed. Chris was holding her, kissing her cheek and neck. She snuggled up to him, covering her lap with her skirt, looking around at the woods, up at the clouds. She looked at me, causing me to blush and concentrate very hard on driving, the car having slowed to a crawl, all by itself.

She laughed. When Chris asked her why, she laughed again and said it was nothing.

Then, with very little persuasion from Chris, she proceeded to toss him off, letting out a little screech when he came—on her, on the seat, on himself. "Hey, Elbert," Chris called. "What's the kleenex situation up there?" "No problem," I croaked, handing him the little travelpack from the console.

What a pair these two were, the proverbial match made in heaven! And there was good old Elbert, practically a participant, an accessory to sex.

Not too long after that, they went all the way, right there in the back seat with the sun shining and the Temptations on the eight-track.

And soon they settled into a favorite routine—it was certainly my favorite.

After making out—kissing, petting, slipping articles of clothing up, down, or off, while I drove out to perhaps the most deserted stretch of country road in southwest Ohio, Jeannie would remove shorts or skirts and panties, then hike her pullover up over her breasts. Chris would by this time have his pants down around his ankles, or off altogether. Jeannie would then straddle Chris and lower herself onto him, not toward him, but facing forward, facing the front of the car, toward me.

Chris liked it that way. He liked to reach around to Jeannie's tits and down between her legs, and he liked to watch her back, her ass.

I didn't object.

She would move around in a sort of circle, sort of wave, or slide up and down oh, so slowly. Early on, she liked the feel of Chris's penis just penetrating, just parting her, then out again. Over and over, ever so slowly.

Soon she would lower herself all the way while Chris cupped a breast with one hand and stroked between her legs with the other. She might attend to the other breast, usually just around the nipple, circling and sort of pinching. Though she sometimes said, "Easy, gentle, Chris," she herself was sometimes not gentle.

Her hair would be blowing back in the breeze. She might ask me to drive slower, or—more often—drive faster. As she worked up toward climax, she liked to feel the wind; she said once that she could feel it on her breasts, her throat and her face, especially her lips, her mouth.

Soon she would ease Chris's fingers out of the way. She'd use the same motions, the same rhythms as the time she'd soloed.

Up and down, up and down, but now down to where she could feel the penis inside her. Back and forth, up and down. Her face would take on a pained look; she'd bite her lower lip, her breath coming in quick little sucking sounds. Her belly would heave, her fingers stop, squeeze and she'd be almost, but not quite still, one hand pressing her lower belly, the other on her breast or on the back of my seat for balance. Twice, I remember, she touched my shoulder.

And sometimes when I'd look up after checking the road...sometimes...I'd look in that mirror and see Jeannie looking at me.

What she was thinking, I don't know, can only imagine. I imagined then and have been imagining on lonely nights or slow afternoons in the years since. But it
really doesn't matter; all that matters is that as she sat
there, fucking Chris in the backseat of my fire-engine
red Wildcat convertible, one hand on the front seat for
balance—my front seat—the other hand working hard
bringing herself to orgasm and beyond—it was me she
was looking at, my eyes into which she gazed. Not
Chris's. Mine.

I saw them only a few times after that summer. In
August they got married and moved 140 miles south to
Lexington, where Chris got a job at Keeneland
Racetrack. I stayed in Dayton and took a position at the
Dayton Daily News. Two years went by.

Then, out of the blue, Chris called me. Asked me to
meet him and Jeannie for lunch at Henrici's, a few
blocks from the paper's garage, my headquarters.

During lunch, a really good hamburger for a change,
we talked about a lot of things—old acquaintances, our
jobs, but not our rides together. Chris was his usual,
pleased-with-the-world self. Jeannie was quiet. But over
coffee, she watched me for a while, and finally asked if
I'd do them a favor. Would I take them for a ride just
for old times' sake?

It took me a minute to get the coffee out of my
lungs, time enough to couch my reply in some
semblance of restraint, calm.

Well, sure, I said. I'd be very pleased, very honored
to, I'd call in sick, no problem. But one problem: who
would want to sit in the back of my beat-up Nova,
printers' ink all over the seats?

Chris said, "That's OK. We'll take our car."

Which turned out to be a virgin white '63 Catalina
ragtop with leather upholstery—bench seat in back
covered with sheepskin, buckets in front, tape deck, a
golden oldies tape sitting on the console next to a

Kleenex travelpack. And the damnedest rearview mirror you've ever seen.

Speed Bumps

Terry Lawhead

— **Oh** no.

— What.

— Speed bumps. Damn I hate 'em. Now we're definitely going to be late.

— It doesn't matter, Thomas.

— Huh. Well, that's news to me, coming from you, who always wants to be there on time.

— Tonight, though, it doesn't matter. Really. Look, we're coming up on another one. Slow down.

— I'm already slowed down. Christ, how many of these things are there?

— Slower. More slow. Slow. There.

— You have got to be kidding.

— Just ease over it. Easy. Yes....Now with — wait! — go slow, yeh, just coast the back tires over...wonderful.

— Wonderful. We'll catch the midnight show, eh? Wasn't this shortcut your idea?

— Yeh it was, sweetheart.

— Hope you're liking it.

— I am.

She sat forward and laid her head on the dash, looking at me, her face softly illuminated in the red glow of the radio and instrument lights, hair tumbling forward over her eyes. She was taking off her shoes.

— Got an itch?

— Yeh.

She slid her underwear down her legs as if taking off something invisible, something only she knew about under her dress which now freed her. She slipped her hand between my legs and held my inner thigh firmly.

—Here comes another one.

—Just take it slow.

She popped my belt buckle and my levis fell apart as I punched my way up through the loose buttons like a magic snake.

—You guys and your soft levis, my god, you should be arrested for indecency, for provocation and harrassment of female intuition. Hit this one hard.

—What?

—Hit this speed bump hard. Faster.

—I pressed down on the gas, we lunged forward, banging over the speed bump, the tool box fell over in the bed of the pickup, and she jerked my levis down to my knees.

—Quite the bump.

—You know, animals sometimes lay next to the asphalt speed bumps at night for the radiant heat coming off them. Kinda like curling up.

—What kind of animals? Here comes another one—wow, look at that! Jesus, is that a cougar? It is! Another one! Jesus, were they lying right on the road?

—Take it hard.

I did. The shocks took the jolt stiffly, and she threw a leg across my waist, billowed out her dress and straddled me, facing past me out the porthole rear window.

—Can you see?

—No. We're going to die.

—C'mon, can you see?

—At twelve miles an hour on this abandoned road? Yeh I can see, I feel my way along, bump to bump.

—She flipped down my shorts, searched for a moment and thrust down hard taking me deep into her body. I clanked into first gear and we slowly rolled along.

—So. Where does this road really take us?

—To the sea.

She was humming softly, moving up and down, pulling her dress up over her head in one movement and brushing warm lips up and down my neck. My own shirt fell open, her lips fluttered like hummingbirds up and down my chest. My nipples exploded, sending annihilating messages to my brain. Two deer leaped up from behind a speed bump and bounded into the dark trees. Mating. The cougars had been mating.

—The sea? What sea?

—The tropical sea. Believe me.

—I do.

—Hit it hard, Thomas.

She began pumping me like I was a shell loading into a twelve gauge, pitching forward and slapping down. Her breasts were hard as a nubile statue layin' in sand, an ancient fantasty. She completely blocked the road. Body scents closed my eyes. I floored it. She inserted her tongue deep inside my ear, inside my brain, short-circuited all nerve endings except those connected to my crotch. We hit the bump, she rose and fell. Then we were cruising on smooth blacktop blindly.

—Hope the animals hear us coming 'cause I can't see a thing.

—They're all fucking, sweet Thomas, this is the night. Slow down.

She pushed her breasts into my face and I gave myself in to sucking and licking.

—Back there in the dark, along the roadside, are animals laying together, moist fur and shiny eyes. All animals purr, Thomas, but they have to be alone. They have to feel safe.

I revved the engine in neutral, popped the clutch, and we squeaked ten feet, slipping sideways a little. I shifted into second, double clutched into third. She was moaning to the whine of the transmission, moving her body like the song of a piano, up and down the scale, up and down, the romantic joyful riff of a smoky barroom filled with laughter and expectation in the face of the beloved. She changed her own movement when I crammed into fourth. I sucked her nipples, wet with my own lips, saw animals leaping out of the way on both sides of her small shoulders — zebras with glittering eyes, monkeys clinging to one another, herons flapping along the ground, necks outstretched, tiny deer — we were plowing through the belly of Noah's ark. Then we weren't touching ground at all. She lifted off my body entirely, sat on my thighs and plunged her mouth onto me as if diving into a pool, coursing right into the center of my body and stretching out, squeezing me everywhere.

Only stars were visible outside the windshield.

Then we landed, on a sandy beach, nose of the truck dipping down first followed by the light bed. I held the gas pedal down, we slipped side to side in the deep sand, just missing palm trees flashing by. I held onto the steering wheel as if we were in a speedboat and she held onto me as if I were her parachute, hands under my rump, face pushed into my lap, sucking.

She came up again, pushed her breasts into my mouth, lay across me, thrust me inside of her again, held onto the back of the seat and rammed me deep into the cushion. I made a guess. The surf was coming up, the sand was wet and hard. I hoped the trees stopped and cranked the wheel to the right. The surf was incandescent off to the left, the horizon was dark before us, the hiss of the receding water flew beneath us.

— You like clams?
— Huh?
— Clams.

She was dripping wet. The smell of the sea filled the

cab. The dash lights were swimming in a fog.

—Clams. Clams. I love clams. The white clam lives 22 years. Shellfish live a long time, a long time. They just filter water, take it in, let it go.

She put her arms under my armpits and galloped.

—I like clams.

—Good.

She sat back and looked at me, her curved body and cascade of hair lit by the dash lights.

—Turn left, sweet Thomas.

I jammed it left and she fell back onto me. We were on a breakwater which had appeared out of nowhere, one narrow lane down the middle. A flashing light was off in the distance, a lighthouse, gulls lifted off around us in clouds of wings, crying their dreamlike song.

—Hard now, Thomas LeRoy, or we will surely die.

I kept the pedal to the metal and my stomach pressed to hers.

—Who owns the sea?

—You do.

She laughed.

—Who owns you?

—The sea.

She began sweeping, long movements, my hands felt her arched rump as she pressed backward, then forward, she was loading the cannon now, stuffing in the ball and powder, pushing it deep down into the shaft, packing it tightly.

The windshield exploded in light as the flash of the lighthouse swept by. She laughed again, raising her head, a dolphin smile gleaming, performing her pelvic dance. A deep purple '52 Chevy pickup worth a year of a working man's wages sped up a landing and was airborne, soaring over a beautiful blue dory tied to a piling. Otters rolled back, eyes wide and glistening, whiskers twitching, interrupted in mating but delighted by the spectacle, the truck against the stars, a parade of

gulls returning to their nests in the boulders, complete
stillness. I cut the engine.

—I can breathe for you.

—I know.

We kissed gently and knifed into the water without a
ripple, like a racer beginning the last leg of the journey,
like a sharp stone thrown by the ecstatic child. The
headlights picked up darting fish, a lumbering tuna, and
as warm water filled the cab, we floated off the seat
buoyant, her hands still clinging to my back and thigh.
We leveled off plunging through the kelp beds, tall
slender plants, and then passed down through the middle of an honor escort of whales, great intelligent heads,
eyes winking in the gleam of the headlights, a matri-
monial aisle of deep mammal love and concern. Far off
was the glow of something big. It looked comforting
and safe.

Author Notes

Loretta Anawalt has had stories in *The New Wave, Slackwater Review* and other publications. She makes her home in Pullman, Washington.

Diana Armstrong works as an editor at the University of Idaho. Her work has appeared in *Palouse Journal, Snapdragon,* and elsewhere. Her book, *Bicycle Camping,* was published by Dial Press (NY). She lives in Moscow, Idaho.

Julia Bowen is a writer and illustrator who makes her home in Idaho.

Olga Broumas lives in Provincetown, Massachusetts, and teaches at Freehand. Her most recent books are *Black Holes, Black Stockings* co-authored with Jane Miller, and *What I Love,* selected translations of Odysseas Elytis. She is currently at work on his essays.

Lin Colson is more than a writer living in Moscow, Idaho.

Pierre Delattre has published two novels: *Tales of a Dalai Lama* and *Walking on Air,* both from Houghton-Mifflin. "Golden Trout" is an excerpt from a third book, *Korrigan's Wedding.* His stories have appeared in *The Atlantic, Harper's Bazaar, Playboy,* and elsewhere. He currently lives in Minnesota.

Sara Donart is a writer and journalist now residing in Eugene, Oregon.

Michael Frome is a noted conservation writer. His most recent book, *Promised Land: Adventures & Encounters in Wild America,* is published by Morrow. He lives in Ashland, Wisconsin.

Jim Goldsmith teaches at Lewis and Clark College in Lewiston, Idaho.

Jackie Kelly is a writer, musician, and massage therapist from Provincetown, Massachusetts.

Terry Lawhead is a writer and editor who now makes his home in Honolulu.

Charlotte Mendez has just published her first novel, *Condor and Hummingbird* (Wild Trees Press), and has had stories in *Ms., North American Review,* and elsewhere. She lives and works in upstate New York.

Susan Moon is a published author and editor living in Berkeley, California.

Joy Passanante is a writer and editor who works from a Moscow, Idaho homebase. She often presents seminars in business writing throughout the state.

Rita Speicher is the author of *Night Lives/Other Lives.* The selection included in this anthology is part of a larger unpublished work titled *Healing Arts After Hours.* She lives in Provincetown, Massachusetts, where she is co-director of Freehand, a fine arts program.

Robert Wrigley has published two books of poems: *The Sinking of Clay City* and *Moon in a Mason Jar.* Other work has appeared in *American Poetry Review* and *Palouse Journal.* He is the 1986 Idaho Writer-in-Residence.

Field Notes

Field Notes

Field Notes

Field Notes

Field Notes

Field Notes